TWO WOMEN
OF GALILEE

TWO WOMEN OF GALILEE

MARY ROURKE

MIRA

ISBN-13: 978-0-7783-2432-4
ISBN-10: 0-7783-2432-X

TWO WOMEN OF GALILEE

www.MIRABooks.com

Printed in U.S.A.

First Printing: March 2006
10 9 8 7 6 5 4 3 2 1

ACKNOWLEDGMENTS

I was helped tremendously in writing this book
by Rafael Luévano, my friend and the first to read each draft.
No one understands the craft of storytelling better than he does.

Laura Dail, my agent, gave her unwavering support,
with extraordinary warmth and courtesy. Joan Marlow Golan
more than lived up to her basic rule of editing, "First, do no
harm." Her suggestions made things better. Joanna Pulcini's
early encouragement set this book in motion. Paddy Calistro
and Scott McAuley at Angel City Press opened doors for me
all along the way and taught me how to turn a printout
into a manuscript. Thank you all.

For Patti, Louis, Tom, Cliff and Jon

The twelve were with him as well as some women
who had been cured of evil spirits and infirmities.
...Joanna, the wife of Herod's steward Chuza...
and many others, who provided for them out of
their own resources.

—*Luke* 8:1-3

The house in Nazareth is empty now. No one would
presume to live there since Mary went away. They
cannot risk inheriting her misfortune, a widow with a crucified son. Still, it is a sacred place. Someone has to oversee its
safekeeping.

As an older woman Mary traveled to distant cities with
John, the youngest of her son's followers, watching over him
like a mother. In those years it was easier to move about the

empire. Claudius ruled from Rome, and for once the foreigner who controlled Judea felt kindly toward the Hebrews.

It is hard to believe, after twelve years of Nero, that such a time ever existed. Jerusalem has been under siege since Passover, and the Roman blockade makes it impossible for food to get beyond the city gates. For us, here in the north, news of the struggle comes with the caravans. The worst of it seems to reach us with the speed of an arrow. There was the man who swallowed his gold before he tried to escape the Holy City. When the soldiers caught him, they sliced him open and pulled the coins from his belly. He was still alive. He witnessed it.

Mary's empty house was my consolation after she went away. I missed her so much that I spent hours there, alone. Imagining she was still with me, I saw things about her I had not noticed before. Her hair, once lavish and dark, had turned the silvery color of a moonstone. Her skin was still the warm shade of an almond shell, but the flash of pink that once tinted her cheeks had faded. The passing years wore her edges smooth as sea glass.

One afternoon in my daydreams she walked past me to the grain cistern, gathered dried kernels in her hands and poured them into storage sacks. She pinched the lice from the nearby bin of ripening grain. Without stopping to greet me, she lifted a clay jug from the shelf and went out toward the well, pausing long enough to look at me contentedly. I heard her whisper the prayers of blessing and I began to recite them with her. Before I met Mary, I did not know any prayers.

In her empty house I started to remember things. There was the scent of rosemary on the cooking pots and the shelf of baskets that waited to be filled with sweet cakes from her kitchen. All of what she owned was worn down with use.

Her small living quarters hardly seemed the sort of place to attract visitors at all hours, but so many came, hoping to gain her favor, that a good number had to be turned away at the gate. Looking back on those bewildering days, I still wonder—did any of us who asked for her help truly understand, or even suspect, what Mary was prepared to do for those she loved? When the time came, she would risk her life. Some might even say, her soul.

One afternoon a shower of dirt interrupted my reverie. It fell from the ceiling of Mary's house, where the roof had worn thin. Above my head, palm fronds whistled like wind chimes in the breeze. I could see them through the holes in the ceiling. Straw poked through the plaster. I hadn't noticed.

To restore such a ruin was my way of honoring Mary, but it was a strange ambition for a woman like me who did not know how to do housework. I, Joanna, wife of Chuza, Herod Antipas's chief steward, was raised to be mistress of an estate. I had little experience with house cleaning or other manual labor. For Mary's sake, I learned.

From the time I made my decision, I began to rise from my bed before the sun lit the upper rooms of my house. Pulling myself from beneath cool linen sheets, I prepared for a day of repair work on Mary's crumbling house. Loading storage baskets with jugs of wine, flasks of oil, perfume bottles, old

jewelry—all items I could exchange for craftsmen's services—
I left the marble gods and colonnades of my Roman-style city
of Sepphoris for the barley fields of eastern Galilee. It was like
traveling backward in time.

Phineas, my driver, covered the three miles in a race against
the sunrise. He had made far more perilous journeys for my
sake during his long years in my service. Never once had he
disappointed me. I therefore rested quietly as he jostled us
toward Nazareth, past brown-faced ewes that stood in the
road and stared, unaccustomed to carriages hurtling past. Not
used, either, to seeing a woman like me, with clean, oval fingernails and pale skin that rarely was subjected to long hours
in the sun.

Closer to the town, field boys pelted my cab with rotten
olives. Phineas growled like a wolf planning an attack, which
kept them at their distance. His smooth eunuch's cheeks and
shining head were set proudly on thick shoulders and massive
arms. He was powerfully made and commanded respect.

As we entered through the Nazareth town gate, the screech
of iron hinges never failed to disturb Mary's neighbors. They
stumbled from their two-room houses or shallow caves to see
who had entered. Their mistrusting expressions asked what
a rich woman was doing in their part of the province. I had
no easy answer. Besides, the smell of sheep on their rough
tunics stiffened my nose. I avoided conversation.

It was on one such morning's drive that I decided to write
about Mary. At first I thought that my own stormy existence
had no place in her story. My failing health, the intrigues at

Herod Antipas's court and the resulting troubles in my marriage did not seem to reveal anything about Mary's ways.

I soon realized that she had guided me through the most intimate events in my life, down to my current situation. There is nothing but to tell our stories as one.

We were cousins. I only discovered it when I was a grown woman and went to see Mary for the first time. I needed her assistance. I was dying and she had a son, a healer who cured desperate cases. I wanted her to arrange a private meeting for me.

My illness had plagued me from childhood. Consumption was part of the Romans' legacy to the East. Caesar's armies carried it with them as they advanced, conquering everything in their path.

My family considered my ailment to be part of the price Judea paid for progress. Stone paved highways and international trade had made my relatives wealthy. Roman sympathizers from long before I was born, they did not consider the life of one daughter too exorbitant a tax on their fortune.

I, however, was not prepared to die for commerce. After many attempts at a complete cure, including one unbearable summer at a health resort near the Dead Sea, my soggy insides refused to dry out.

As my last hope, I turned to Mary. I was prepared to reward her handsomely. I have always been a woman of means.

CHAPTER ONE

And laying his hands on each one, he healed them.

—*Luke* 4:38

Consumption found me, unsuspecting, on my twelfth birthday. That morning my father granted my wish and took me boating on the open sea despite the winter cold and my mother's protests. I was willful, even as a girl.

I rushed toward my fate in a dart across the water. My father's dark reed boat cut through the chilled air as he pounded a mallet on a wooden block. The oarsmen strained to keep pace. I saw my father smiling and felt proud to be so much like him.

The wind in my hair and the flutter inside me made me lurch from my place and run to chase the waves. Leaning out of the boat for a whitecap, I lost my balance and fell overboard.

It was a sea of melted snow. Two oarsmen dove to save me,

and after a few minutes of reaching for oars, clinging to ropes that were hoisting us up, we were rescued. But my shivering started right away and would not stop. After I spent weeks in a dark room beneath blankets heated by warm stones, the doctor told my parents what I am sure they already knew.

All of my father's money could not buy back my health. I survived, and recovered for the most part, but in cold weather I rattled from the wet congestion that welled up inside me. If I grew agitated or afraid, it was almost impossible to breathe. For years afterward, my strength would come and go. The doctors prescribed sailing in the open air as a way to balance my humors and soothe me. This remedy helped to quiet my hacking on warm summer days, but the benefits never lasted long.

Finally, after I was married, my illness threatened to defeat me. The only way I managed to keep up with my husband's pace was by resting for long months at our home in Sepphoris. His demanding life took us there several times each year, although Herod Antipas, the Tetrarch of Galilee and my husband's superior, had moved the seat of his government from Sepphoris to Tiberias. Both cities were essential to the life of the province. Both had been rebuilt in the Roman style, during Antipas's early years in power.

He did it to please the Romans. He always imagined that if he ruled his small northern territory to their liking, one day they would place him in charge of far larger regions.

Fortunately, Antipas preferred the new capital and my husband preferred the old, in part because it kept him away from court for a good part of the year. Tiberias was exciting to Antipas. Aside from my husband's sensible urge to avoid the tetrarch as much as possible, he and I both favored Sepphoris for sentimental reasons. It is the city where I was raised and where Chuza and I first met.

During one of our seasons at home, we planned an evening at the theater with Manaen, Chuza's young colleague. I was glad to have my husband seen with the young captain of the guard. Manaen had grown up with the tetrarch, although he was nearly half his age, and was favored at court. Lately Antipas had asked my husband to teach Manaen about accounting and agriculture, essential for a young man's promotion.

I wanted to make a good impression and so commissioned a pottery vase as a memento of our evening, to impress upon Manaen that my husband approved of him. On the morning of our engagement I went to the garden to see that the glaze had fully dried in the sun.

An unexpected coolness in the air sent a chill across my shoulders, and I began to cough. As my handkerchief became speckled with blood, I felt Chuza's hands lifting me up. "Keep breathing," he said. He behaved like a general at such times. "Lift your head off your chest." The rosebushes tilted sideways as Strabo, my chief gardener, and two house servants lifted me and carried me indoors. "Don't call the doctor," I shouted at Chuza. "Please, just stay with me."

He followed the servants to my rooms, and once I was settled on my couch, he sat near me. When I was able to breathe quietly, he lay down beside me. He always wanted to stay very close after one of my attacks. They were among the few things in life that could frighten him.

I looked at his face, so near to mine. His hair, thick as a bear's coat, showed the first receding signs of age. His jaw had lost none of its square features. To feel his broad chest against me filled me with loneliness. We seldom touched anymore. He seemed afraid that I might shatter and break.

"Chuza," I whispered.

For a time we lay quietly together.

"Tell me about when we first met."

He answered in a low voice. "It's been seventeen years this spring." My husband always remembered anniversaries better than I did. "I was supposed to be on my way to Corinth, delivering a shipment of gold bound for Rome. But the winds had shifted and we could not sail. It was one of the first warm nights in March. I walked to the colonnade and discovered that everyone in Sepphoris had the same idea. That is when I first saw you." He kissed my nose, as he used to do when we were young and first getting to know each other.

Chuza did call his doctors soon enough. They advised me to stay home, rest and spend time in the sun. Sun to brown my arms like a farmer's wife, home to starve me of the latest gossip.

My husband sent to Antioch for his brother, Cyrus, one of the finest doctors in their native city. Within hours of his arrival I was lying in my bed, hugging a beaker of some gritty concoction of his, trying everything I knew to avoid the smoldering prod he held near me. Cyrus believed that cauterizing was the best treatment for my ailment.

He seemed to think he could roast my congestion to a powder. I let him try. It may have helped. I did seem to improve for a time, but I had learned not to trust my reprieves. There was no reason to expect a cure.

Several days later, after a few glasses of the herbal brew that was part of Cyrus's treatment, I felt surprisingly healthy. Octavia, my maidservant, who sat with me in my rooms that morning, paused from her mending to make a suggestion. She could see that I was stronger than I had been in some time.

"There is a caravan from the East passing through town," she said. Her eyebrows spread across her forehead, dark as a blackbird's wings. Arched in that way, they warned me that Octavia had plans for us. It was pointless to argue, she was as confident about her opinions as anyone. She had not been born to be a servant—it was only her father's gambling that had ruined her future. He sold her to pay off his debts.

We set out to hunt for peppercorns and perhaps a jewelry box covered with tiny mirrors like the one Antipas's wife, Herodias, owned. By early afternoon we were walking along the alleys between the stalls in Sepphoris. Silvery cranes squawked at us from their cages, the bitter scent of leather wafted from the sandal maker's shop, sacks of black tea opened to my touch and I rolled the crisp leaves between my fingers.

At first the rumbling behind me sounded like exotic drumming. Caravans are filled with foreign music. But the sound grew louder and moved closer until I realized it was the noise of the crowd. People were stampeding behind a man with spindle legs who tottered through the alley. He was old, but he moved like a baby taking his first steps. I had seen him before; it took me a moment to place him. The crippled beggar, we had passed him at the city gate. Somehow, he was walking toward me. A mob crushed around him. "Zorah is cured!" they shrieked. "The healer from Nazareth saved him."

Octavia broke through the crowd and pulled me away from the stalls.

"Where are we going?" I asked, but I could not hear above the roar. Past the tiny yellow flowers that framed the main road, Octavia led and I followed. When we reached a grassy hillside, I looked down at the crowd shambling onto the slope below us like wounded animals. The stronger carried the maimed on their backs. It was as if half the world were coming there to die.

I recognized one woman. She had recently been healed, I'd been told. We all know one another's business in the Galilee. For eight years this woman was possessed by demons. She often lapsed into fits and fell on the ground, her body rigid as a corpse.

She wore a fine woolen cloak colored by the most expensive shellfish dye. Our paths rarely crossed. She was a devout Jew. "Good woman," she called to me. "Jesus can help you, he helped me."

I looked into her eyes and saw no pain in them. She was cured of her illness. I could tell by the way she walked, upright and strong rather than bent in anticipation. She pointed my way down the hill toward the healer. We approached him, and he turned as if he heard someone calling his name. He looked directly at me.

From a distance all I could see was his dark hair and his long, narrow features. There was such compassion in his manner that I could not take my eyes from him.

I went a few steps closer for a better view. His hair curled as gently as a baby's. His lips were longer than any I'd ever noticed. His eyes were as dark as the pool where Narcissus first discovered his own beauty. I knew that this man would listen to me and understand.

Something held me back. It was too sudden——I was not sure what might happen if I got close to him. What if he refused me in front of all those people? What if I was the unlucky one who got worse, not better, because of him?

Pulling away, I rushed toward the road, shouting for my manservant, Phineas. He found me quickly and led me to my litter. I hid there with the curtains drawn shut and ordered Octavia to walk very close by until we were well outside the city. He would have healed me that very day, I am certain. If only I had trusted him. The heart is a timid hunter when it does not yet know what it seeks.

I was so disturbed by my near encounter in Sepphoris that I looked forward to returning to Tiberias. Chuza and I left for the capital several days after my ordeal. One of our first nights, my husband and I attended a birthday party for Herod Antipas. It was an effort to get dressed, knowing what a show of false gaiety the evening would require. I tossed aside six pairs of earrings before settling on gold hoops. They looked as ostentatious as the others, but time demanded that I make a choice.

"Are you ready?" Chuza called from the atrium. I could picture him, rapping his fingers against the wall. A quick glance in my mirror restored my confidence. I smiled at my rolling brown hair that was wrapped, just so, around a headband as slim as a new moon.

"Coming," I answered in a pretended rush.

He smiled as I walked toward him with a swish of frothy drapery. My dress was copied after the statute of Venus in Antipas's garden. Chuza's attentions lifted the clouds that had settled above me.

We walked the stone pathway to Antipas's palace. It was a lesson in the labors that support a royal life. Eight solid gold lanterns shaped like papyrus blossoms lit our way. Egyptian imports, I could tell by the blocky shapes. A team of craftsmen had taken at least six weeks to complete the set. Crossing the mosaic carpet of blue-tipped pheasants in the reception area, I guessed the number of workers needed to install the floor; one to engineer it, as many as nine to lay it in, for a period of not less than two months.

On the way through the house a servant who knew us well allowed us a side trip to the dining room. Antipas had flamboyant tastes and liked his guests to compliment him. I wanted to be prepared.

The room was transformed under a gauzy tent that fluttered from the ceiling. Trapeze bars hovered above the dining couches, hinting at the night's entertainment. I felt my skin tingle in revolt. I could already guess what had been planned.

Chuza led me away, tripping over a dancing monkey as we left the room. The chattering creature screamed at us and chased us down the hall past murals of Bacchus and his tipsy friends, their faces buried in their goblets. My husband kept a protective arm around me, sensing, as I had, what the tent and decor implied. Rome's most famous transvestite, Flavia, was to be the special guest of the evening. My husband did not approve of parties meant for the officers' club. Not when women were present.

In the garden, Antipas stood beside his wife, Herodias, who leaned possessively against him. My eyes went directly to the imperial ring he wore, the one he used for sealing Roman documents. It seemed an intentional show of his authority. His thinning brown hair was crowned with a laurel wreath. I'd never seen him act a closer imitation of a Caesar. Ambition rose off him like an unattractive odor. He was fifty-six years old that night and noticeably eager to secure a higher position in Caesar's inner circle.

"Joanna, you're here at last," he said, a bit too familiar. Chuza ignored it. He was accustomed to Antipas's awkward attempts as a ladies' man.

"My Lord Tetrarch." I gave him an inflated title.

He embraced Chuza like a favorite brother. Antipas had so few real friends that he made more of trusted colleagues than was appropriate.

I listened quietly, until he chose to speak to me. "Tell me the news of my kingdom," he said, leaning toward me. "I know everything about how to rule Galilee but never enough about the people I govern." He moved slightly away from his wife to suggest that I was at liberty to be frank. "She's not interested in such matters," he said, casting a glance toward her.

Their marriage was a complicated arrangement. Her grandfather was Antipas's father, Herod the Great. She abandoned her first husband for Antipas and he put aside a perfectly acceptable wife. It was a messy display, ripe for gossip. Herodias wanted a more powerful husband than the one she had. Antipas simply wanted everything that he did not already own. His incestuous marriage to Herodias infuriated the Hebrews in his court, although he was one of them in name at least. The fact is, his family converted. He would never be fully a Hebrew, as his mother was a Samaritan woman. He had ignored the marriage laws just as he did all the others that got in his way.

I took a small silver rabbit from my pocket, a lucky charm from my afternoon shopping, and showed it to Antipas. He and I had one thing in common. Magic excited us. It was a faithless woman's answer to divine intervention.

"There is a new man in Galilee," I said. "Everyone is talking about him."

"His name, tell me his name."

"Jesus, from Nazareth."

"Who?" His voice cracked. Competition made him wild.

"He is the center of attention."

"What does he do?" Antipas rubbed the lucky rabbit in the palm of his hand.

"He heals the sick." I told the story of Zorah, the cripple.

"And what about you, Joanna?" Antipas turned on me with syrupy concern. "Did the healer from Nazareth cure you?" The words pricked. I forced myself to clear my throat. It was enough to send him away.

After dinner, the lamps were turned down. I could hear the acrobats enter. When they were in their places the torches were lit. Clowns as tall as camels hobbled around the room on wooden stilts. An Ethiopian in a red turban tossed streamers from the back of an elephant. I caught one and tied it around my wrist. From across the room, where the men were seated, I noticed Chuza watching me from the corners of his eyes. I could read his testy expression. He had not approved of my telling Antipas about my day with the wonder-worker, which could only upset the jealous tetrarch.

By the time Flavia rolled onto the trapeze bar, some of the men in the room had been drinking for three hours. They started howling as the performer's golden hair swung over their tables, flitting across their faces. Flavia's painted lips and the black kohl outlining his eyes made him a freakish version of a woman.

He was supple as kelp, twisting into knots, rolling into a ball. Not once did he miss a coin purse tossed his way. It became a game, and like children we got overly excited as we played. A fight broke out. Wine from a flying cup sprayed the side of my face. Chuza stood up abruptly, came and took my arm. "We're leaving," he said. My husband hardly spoke to Antipas on our way out. The tetrarch was pressed against his wife's thick neck and waved us off.

At times the excesses of court life grated against Chuza's soul. Antipas's party was such a time. When we were safely home and settled, my husband came to my room as he sometimes did when he needed consolation. He held me in his arms until his tense body relaxed and grew heavy and his grip loosened. I felt him sleeping and soon, too, I began to drift off.

I found myself thinking about the day I first saw Jesus. The idea came to me then, effortless as the best plans do. "I must go to meet his mother," I said out loud in the dark.

Chuza would not like it. "Joanna," he would say, "don't test the gods." He didn't believe in healers. Only women and fools listened to any of them.

CHAPTER TWO

Mary treasured all these things in her heart.

—*Luke* 2:51

In early autumn, my husband and I returned from Tiberias to Sepphoris for the harvesting of the figs and dates. I had plenty to do at home. We had been away all summer. My roses needed tending.

Our first morning at home I saw my husband off, waited until I was certain he was on his way and called Octavia. "We're going to Nazareth," I said. "We'll need a sack of flour and a jar of olive oil. Add the rest of the salted fish if there is any."

"Doesn't the healer we saw in Sepphoris come from there?" Octavia asked. My maidservant was uncommonly skilled at guessing my intentions.

"I would like to meet his mother," I said. "I don't know her, of course. And perhaps she won't be at home."

"We can wait for her," Octavia suggested. "Or, leave word that we will return another day."

"You like this idea, don't you?" I teased. At times Octavia seemed more like family than a servant.

She widened her dark eyes in approval of my plan. An hour later Phineas was driving us toward Nazareth. The weather was warm and dry. We rolled up the sides of the canopy so that Octavia and I could take in the view. There were several hours of daylight ahead of us and Chuza would not be home until late. Still, I urged Phineas to hurry. We arrived well before dusk and walked the final distance from the town gate so as not to disturb the residents of Nazareth with a horse-drawn carriage.

I hid my hair beneath a sheer white stole, the closest I had to the brown flax of the local women. Fortunately, I had removed my ankle bracelets and left them at home. No one in Nazareth wore such things. Phineas walked close to me, my vigilant bodyguard. He watched the streets from beneath his hooded eyes.

We found Mary sitting on a low wooden bench outside her house, surrounded by the girls from the village who were bubbling with expectation. The youngest of them nestled in their older sisters' arms. Mary passed a bowl of mashed olives and bits of bread to share. She had tied her head scarf at the back of her neck, like a worker in the field. Under her belt she had tucked squares of old fabric that she used to wipe away the crumbs from the younger girls' cheeks. They all went to her and pressed their tiny lips toward her. Anything to get her attention.

Some of the mothers helped to prepare the girls for a story. They dressed the children up as characters, rubbing ash on the faces of those who would play the penitents. Their job, mothers reminded them, was to pray for victory before the battle.

One of the older girls stepped forward and waited until everything was quiet. Then she glanced at Mary, who lifted her chin, just slightly, and nodded her approval. The girl announced the story, "Joshua at the battle of Jericho," and began her narration.

Some of the girls, the defenders of justice, stole into the midnight valley as Mary stretched a line of painted wooden stars above their heads. They marched around the city walls to frighten their enemy, the Cananites. Mary handed a ram's horn to a pudgy girl with one wandering eye. The sudden blast from the horn made the audience lurch into nervous laughter.

When the brave marched back home after their victory, the youngest girls, who had been crowding behind Mary, jumped up. Each one wore a straw wreath in her hair. Mary tapped a tambourine against her hand and led them in the victory dance. The girls imitated her, twirling and spinning as she did.

When they were finished with their story, the more forward girls smiled confidently at the audience, while the shy types clung to Mary's skirt. She bent down and kissed their hair, or whispered words of encouragement.

I practiced my speech, waiting for her to come toward me. She finally did approach, but only after all the mothers and grandmothers had their fill of her attention.

"Peace be upon you," she said to me. She was inviting, as if she thought she knew me.

I thanked her for her blessing, unsure of how to address her. I rarely spoke to people outside my own circle of acquaintances.

"How did you like our story?" she asked.

"I must have heard it when I was young."

"The Lord is always with us. Joshua's victory reminds us of that."

Her confident voice soothed me. "Yes," I said.

I was about to explain my visit when an unusual shyness came over me. I stood looking at her tapered fingers, so like her son's.

"You are Joanna, Abijah's daughter," she said.

"How did you know?"

Her answer was far from what I expected.

"Don't you remember me?" she asked. "I am your cousin."

I can only imagine the expression on my face. Not certain whether to believe her, I tried to appear composed, but the sudden rumbling in my chest betrayed me. My face felt hot and moist. She recognized my illness but did not back away from me, as so many do. Instead, Mary took my arm and walked with me to the low wall that had been crowded with relatives and neighbors not long ago.

"I will bring you something," she said. When I was alone and waiting for her to return, a tickling in my throat worried me. I never knew what a coughing fit might bring. She came back quickly and held out a drink of herbs and honey. It quieted me at last.

"I remember you as a little girl, in the square in Sepphoris," she said. "I would see you there with your parents. Don't you know me? I am the daughter of Joachim and Ann."

My father's brother was Joachim. I was surprised that I recognized the name. I remembered that he had married my mother's sister, Ann. I was very young at the time. Our families broke apart after that. My aunt and uncle kept the Hebrew ways and opposed the Romans, but my father and mother did not. They welcomed Caesar and the wider world he represented. Prosperity became their god.

"You wore pretty woven sashes around your dresses," I recalled. I hadn't thought of my cousin's colorful linen belts for years. "If we saw you in the market, my mother told me I was not to talk to you."

"I envied the way your father carried you in his arms," Mary said. "You were his little treasure."

"And now you have grown children of your own," I said, hoping to ease conversation toward the purpose of my visit.

I didn't know about my cousin's life, only that she was married and her husband died. She raised children with him and called them all her sons and daughters.

"I have seen your son, the healer," I said.

Her gaze moved slowly across my waxy complexion and slid over the coat that hung on my shoulders. "What have you heard about him?"

"That he heals the sick by touching them."

"And so you have come here," she said. Her voice dropped, just slightly. I sensed her caution.

"Perhaps you could arrange for us to meet," I suggested.

"In private, you mean," Mary said.

It suddenly occurred to me that I was not the first to make this request of her.

"My husband is chief steward," I said, to remind her of my station. "It would be awkward if I were to be seen in the crowd that follows your son."

The truth is, I didn't plan to listen to the speeches or learn the teachings of Jesus. I only wanted him to save my life. Mary's silence told me that she understood all of this.

I looked up at the sky to avoid her questioning gaze. A full moon slid from behind the clouds and lit the town, turning whitewashed huts into blue pearls.

It seemed best to end our conversation and continue it another time. My cousin was protective of her son, or, perhaps she did not agree that I deserved special treatment. A moment's shame came over me, an uncommon thing for the wife of Herod's steward.

"May I come to see you again?" I asked. Mary pressed my cold hands between hers, which were strong and reassuring. She did not explain her earlier reticence and I did not dare to ask about it. For all her quiet grace, I sensed a formidable nature.

"I hope you will come to see me again," she said. "You are welcome here."

Octavia had been sitting a close distance from us. I motioned for her to call Phineas. Mary waited with me until he arrived. We were just about to leave when she made a promise. "I will tell my son about you."

CHAPTER THREE

My soul yearns, even faints
For the courts of the Lord

—*Psalms* 84:1

Spring brought the rain that forced the crocus into bloom and the feast of Passover that set the Hebrews on pilgrimage. Each year they entered Jerusalem in such numbers that every rooftop was rented two or three times over. By night the hills outside the city flickered with campfires.

That year Antipas's knees and ankles swelled to twice their normal bulk. He was in such pain from his gout that he could not walk. Chuza went to Jerusalem in the tetrarch's place, to keep order during the festival. I arranged for us to transport my husband's bed, his copy of Virgil and his most comfortable sandals, hoping to lift the gloom out of the guest rooms in the governor's compound where we would stay. Pontius Pilate governed Jerusalem and Judea with disdain for those he ruled. It soured the very air around him, even in his own household.

From the day that we arrived in Jerusalem my husband made a point of being visible on the streets, especially in the Hebrew quarter. At home he turned quarrelsome and complained about things he could usually ignore.

"Give back those berries," he snarled one night at dinner. Manaen, my husband's trusted colleague, was our only guest. Chuza drank several extra glasses of wine, and then he craved something sweet. He reached for the small bowl of wild strawberries, a gift from Claudia Procula, the governor's wife.

"You've had enough," I said. "You know what will happen." Berries raked through Chuza's insides like shattered glass. I slid the bowl away from him.

"Tell me," Manaen interrupted. "What have you seen around the city these last few days?" Manaen was at least ten years younger than my husband, closer to my age. He spoke with the respect he would show a teacher. Chuza warmed to it.

"Chaos," my husband said, tossing back another swallow of wine. "You would think Tiamat and his demons had taken control."

"The Syrian god," I offered. "The one who rebelled against heaven." My husband's references to his native gods were always from the old regime. It was his way of mocking the whole idea of a heaven and an underworld. He didn't believe in gods any more than I did. He therefore called on those who had been cast out after the Greeks conquered Syria.

Manaen nodded politely, not much interested in my help.

"I have seen it, of course," he said about the frenzied crowds.

"Does it offend you, that the Jews are patrolled this way?" Chuza asked. "You are one of them, after all."

"I'd rather it be me keeping order in the streets than someone who has no understanding of them." Our guest was a clever politician.

"The city swells to three times its normal size during Passover, as you know," my husband said. "You can help by re-assuring the Jews that the Romans only want to keep the peace."

They were at ease with each other in a way I rarely saw in either of them when Antipas was present. They talked about how to relieve traffic near the temple and limit the fire hazards in the campsites outside the city. I stole glances at Manaen's amber-colored hair, his green eyes.

"We had to stop repairs on the aqueducts as of this morning," Chuza said, swizzling the last of his wine. "It's the worst possible time for it. After all the rain, the plaster is peeling off the canals." Every year at Passover, what Pilate resented most was the work stoppage. He had no choice.

"The Hebrews don't work on their holy days," Manaen said. "I am only here because it is my duty. Antipas has never asked me before."

"It's pointless to force them when so many refuse to coop-erate," Chuza said. "Nearly half the men working on the aqueducts now are Jews. Pilate gives in to them for one reason. He expects them to give him seven days of peace in return. No riots."

"Bribery," Manaen said. An outspoken man, he must get noticed at court, I thought as I guessed the width of his shoulders. Nearly double that of his waist. He ran his fingers absently over the leather cuff he wore on his wrist.

"There have been riots, you know," I said, looking to my husband for approval. "That was before you were born, Manaen."

"Some of the worst were more than thirty years ago," Chuza said. "Oddly enough, they were in Sepphoris." He sat forward on his couch, more interested now that the conversation turned to war stories. "Herod the Great sent soldiers to inspect the city, with Caesar's insignia blazing on their shields. It's against Jewish laws to make a human replica."

"Idolatry," Manaen answered.

"They stoned the soldiers and forced a retreat. The next day Herod sent five hundred men into Sepphoris. They torched the city. Hundreds were killed." Excited by this talk of military strategy, Chuza reached across the table, scooped up a few more berries and tossed them into his mouth.

Manaen picked up the story. "There were no Hebrews in Sepphoris for some time after that. Not until Herod the Great died and Antipas was named Tetrarch of Galilee."

"That's right. Antipas brought them back." Chuza was delighted by all this talk of blood and battles. "He needed workers to rebuild the city and they needed jobs. Why not bring them back? He is a Jew himself, though he doesn't keep their ways. I give him credit. The city has improved its relations with the Romans, over time."

Finishing the last of his wine, Chuza placed his cup on the table. In the same move he dropped a few more berries into his mouth, looked at me and smiled sweetly.

He knew what I was about to say and so answered me, "They will not." I went to sit beside him on his couch. His drooping eyelids told me he was tired. I nudged him to his feet and aimed him toward the door.

"I'll take the first shift in the morning," Manaen said, rising in respect for my husband. He was taller than Chuza by a hand's width.

"May I go with him?" I asked. Chuza stopped our swaying walk and puffed up his cheeks to hold back a laugh.

"I've always wondered," I said, pushing away the berry bowl as we passed by the table, "what it is like in the temple precinct at the festival." Perhaps I would see the healer from Nazareth. His mother might have told him about me, as she promised.

Chuza reached around me. His fingers danced mischievously along the rim of the berry bowl. Life with him was a game of negotiations. He did not reach for more but passed the table and went toward Manaen. "A woman from court is never welcome in the temple precinct," he said. "It will make your work more difficult."

"She'll be all right with me," Manaen said.

Chuza slapped his young friend on the shoulders and shook him. Then, he came back to me, reached behind me and scooped the last of the berries into his mouth.

"Good," he said, content that he was getting his way. "Now we can all go to bed happy."

The next morning at sunrise Manaen appeared rested but not relaxed. His eyes seemed screwed tighter in their sockets.

"We'll pass by the outskirts of the campsite on our way to the temple," he said over his shoulder. Eight armed guards followed us. I covered my hair with a scarf I had draped over my shoulders.

The vest Manaen had chosen for our tour worried me. Studded leather, it was the sort worn by hunters.

"Do you expect trouble?" I asked.

"Caution can prevent problems."

As we came closer to the campsite, he led us along the outskirts, traveling at a respectful distance from the Hebrews. Some of the tents we passed were made of canvas and set up precisely, others were a balancing act of wooden planks and striped blankets. It was not unlike the villages near Sepphoris.

At a cooking fire three women built up the morning embers with pine needles and fallen branches that the children carried in from the thickets. Two cauldrons of porridge hung from iron stakes over the heat. One woman was making bread on a large stone.

New pilgrims came trailing into the camp from the hills to the north. Even before I could see them, I heard their chant.

Happy are those who live in your house,
Ever singing your praise.
Happy are those whose strength is in you,
In whose heart are the highways to Zion.

Out of the crowd, a woman ran toward us. I thought she was hurrying to tell the men who were tending the herd nearby that new people were arriving. But she swerved suddenly, rushed directly at me and spat at my cloak.

"Give that to your Governor Pilate," she snarled as she raced back toward the camp.

"Bring that woman here," Manaen ordered, his voice hard as iron.

"Can't we just go on?" I said, wiping the spit off without looking.

Two guards reached the woman quickly and scooped her up as if she were a mole plucked by an owl. They dragged her to Manaen and dropped her in front of him. A crowd had gathered to watch what would happen. Manaen met their hostile stares.

"Take her away," he said to the guards.

The woman dropped her forehead to the dirt and wailed as two men from our escort tied her hands with rope.

We moved on.

"It's not the worst thing," Manaen said, his eyes locked on the view ahead of us. "Plenty of troublemakers are put in jail and released after the festival."

I found myself defending the woman. "She did what many of her people would like to do to those who betrayed them and followed the Romans," I said. "My ancestors were treated like royalty for their support, while our relatives lost everything."

"Why did your father, born a Hebrew, support the Romans?" Manaen asked, impatient as if he were talking to a dull child.

"He said Rome could bring our backward country into the modern world."

"He was right."

"Do you like seeing the Romans in control?"

"We can't push progress out of our way. The Caesars bring progress."

I watched his face for anything that might explain the anger mixed with a fatherly concern in his voice. It was only clear to me that he had conflicted emotions about the Romans.

"Onward," he shouted. The soldiers closed in behind us and followed.

We rode to the temple precinct in silence. When we were almost there, I asked if we could give up our horses and walk.

"Too dangerous," Manaen said. "I promised your husband that I would protect you, and the crowds are unpredictable."

I tried flattery. "But you can handle them," I said. He did not waver.

At the archway leading to the gentiles' court we finally did dismount and stepped into an explosion of noisy activity. The merchant stands on the plaza were buried under a crush of customers haggling for votive candles and frescoed tablets painted with scenic views of the temple. Butchers selling sheep and goats from wooden carts could not move the squealing beasts fast enough.

The entire courtyard pulsed with life—pilgrims, caged doves, money changers' booths. The stench of bloody hides mixed with the more pleasant scent of incense. Two herders passed us with a carcass tied to a pole that rested between their shoulders. The bulging eyes of the animal's head grazed my nose. I gagged. The cough I had been stifling broke out. I had to turn away and try to hide my fit from my escort. Blood speckled my handkerchief, but I was skilled at making light of my attacks. I drank water from the skin I wore at my hip and breathed slowly until at last I regained my composure.

As the herders passed the alms box, one of them dropped the pole and placed his coins in the slot. An older man tripped on the beast and fell. Some weasel-faced character rushed to help him and deftly slipped the old man's change purse off his belt. Spinning on his toes, the pickpocket stood face-to-face with Manaen, who caught him by the neck.

"You're going to jail," he snarled, motioning for the guards to remove the oily thief. I took a step backward as the old man staggered to his feet, his forehead smeared with blood. He fell against Manaen, who steadied the frail body. I took another step back. I could hear the voices of the women praying in their separate court. They were closer than before.

An energetic father and his little boy cut across my path, dragging their goat toward the butcher's stone inside the men's court. Their lips moved in exact harmony as they recited the blessing. I took another step back to give them room.

"Wait there," Manaen ordered me, maneuvering around the goat without taking his eyes off me.

A barefoot priest spattered with blood hurried across the plaza. In his rush toward the sanctuary he kicked a jar of oil that someone had left behind. It frightened a young boy, who dropped his lighted candle. The flame ignited the oil.

People scattered.

I ran to the end of the wide courtyard and all but threw myself into the women's quarters. Men were forbidden from entering, and Manaen could not reach me there. Veiled heads turned toward me to see who was disrupting the prayers. I kept my face hidden and made my way to the back. I began to follow the other women's movements. They were like dancers, bowing low, reaching toward the heavens.

Could prayer heal me? I wondered.

The scent of sandalwood filled my nose and made me light-headed. A tickle in my throat refused to be stilled. I breathed evenly, trying to calm myself. Slowly my insides settled. The voices of the women near me, chanting their prayer, lulled me as if I were an infant falling sleep.

More at peace than I had been in some time, I relaxed and listened. It was then that I heard a distinct voice. It was huge and loud enough to shake the temple walls, yet it felt very close. I wondered if it came from somewhere inside me. I heard my name. "Joanna."

I searched the sky for thunderheads, but only white clouds drifted by.

The echoing voice filled me like the sound of a ringing bell. Some force, more enormous than Mount Horeb, called to me again.

"Joanna."

"God of my ancestors," I said. I can't explain how I knew who it was.

"Help me!" I cried. "I don't want to die."

Two thick hands clamped onto my shoulders. The women had finished their prayers and emptied the courtyard without my noticing. Manaen was standing beside me, prodding me toward the main courtyard. Glaring, he pressed his fingers into my arm and directed me quickly out of the place forbidden to all men. His embarrassment made him even angrier.

"You put yourself and my men in danger." He clenched his teeth so tightly they should have splintered.

"I had to see for myself. You wouldn't have agreed to it."

"This isn't a contest of wills," he shouted. "I can't protect you unless you follow the rules."

His shoulders slowly fell back to their usual position. "When your husband finds out, he will not like this."

CHAPTER FOUR

His mother said…"do whatever he tells you."

—*John* 2:5

Crumpled on my bed, alone and confused, I sank into a dreamy sleep. From a place near the window, a narrow figure of a man came toward me. He was carrying a physician's box. One of Chuza's doctors, I supposed. Rolling back the sleeve of his robe, he uncovered his long fingers and pressed them against my cheek. The warm impression lingered, like a blessing. He placed his hand upon me, a hand so large it formed a collar around my throat. His touch freed my labored breathing. I thought I knew him but could not recall where we met. Opening my eyes, I expected to see him beside me. He was gone.

"Chuza," I called, drowsiness weighting my voice. I went

from room to room searching for my husband, until I realized it was midday and he was not at home. Octavia prepared a bath with chamomile, where I steeped until I heard him coming along the hall. His thick leather sandals padded his heavy steps. Dressing quickly I met him as he entered my rooms.

"Manaen told me what happened this morning," he said. He was stern and unapproachable.

"We got separated at the temple."

"Separated? You ran away from him. Joanna, you knew it was dangerous."

"Something happened to me, Chuza."

"You could have caused a riot. You put my men in danger."

Leaning against the window behind me, I moved my fingers along the sill like a blind woman feeling her way.

"I wanted to pray."

"You promised to stay with Manaen."

"I knew I was safe."

"Joanna."

Chuza's disappointment melted my confidence.

"What will Pilate say?" he murmured. "And of course Antipas will hear all about it, if he hasn't already."

"Someone called my name. I heard a voice."

"Manaen is one of our best men. He could have been slaughtered by that crowd."

The sound of a heavy object dropping on a hard surface came from the next room. Chuza hurtled in that direction. There was Octavia, sitting at my writing table, cleaning ink bottles and pens.

"You can go," I said. She hurried away without trying to explain herself.

"I forgot she was here," I said. "I trust Octavia, she is very loyal."

My husband looked out at the tile roof across the courtyard that sheltered the rooms where Antipas stayed when he was in Jerusalem. On the rise of the next hill was Pilate's villa. Chuza's reputation, his honor, depended on their certainty that he was a strong leader. I saw my actions through his eyes. They were inexcusable, yet I tried once more to explain.

"God called my name this morning," I said.

"No one will believe that," Chuza answered. "God is a social obligation, not someone who talks to people."

"We don't have to tell anyone."

"After the spectacle you made of yourself this morning? Everyone in Jerusalem knows." Chuza's short thick hands flying in the air above his head told me he was as angry as I had ever seen him.

"Maybe no one will mention it," I whimpered, hoping to win his forgiveness.

"That's what spies are for."

I was not helping matters, and Chuza was not really listening.

"I have to lie down," I said. My husband left me.

Of all the plans that came to me when I was alone, only one brought comfort. I called Octavia and asked her to find Phineas, my driver. He entered my sitting room, bowing slightly.

"Go to Nazareth in the morning," I instructed him. It was a long trip. He would be gone at least seven days, yet my good servant did not flinch.

"Tell no one here where you are going. When you reach Nazareth, find the healer's mother and ask if I might visit her twelve days from now." I took a small stone jar of rose water from my dressing table and gave it to him as a gift for her.

The next day Pilate and his wife invited us to the governor's palace to celebrate the end of the Jewish festival. Chuza escorted me to the women's quarters on his way to join the men. Of all the women at court, Pilate's wife, Claudia Procula, was the only one I ever much liked. For some reason she took to me, as well. I suppose it was that we could talk for hours about our astrologers and the excitement of luck and chance.

I believed that wonder-workers were my best hope for an end to my illness. It was a matter of stumbling upon the right one. As for Procula, the pressures of her husband's high rank gave her endless reasons to seek the advice of the soothsayers.

In her airy apartment on the second floor of the palace, Procula bounced from guest to guest. For such a large woman she was unusually light on her feet, balancing wide, rolling curves of flesh above her small, dainty shoes. She fussed over us, passing bowls of plump raisins and braided bread flavored with almonds. I recognized it, a family recipe from home. Cordoba, was it? I'd never been to a party at the governor's palace that did not include almond bread.

As I crossed the room I began to notice that the other women were watching. When I passed the dessert table three of them covered their faces to hide their laughter. I knew it was at my expense.

An older woman sat alone in the corner nodding to the sounds of a harp. I passed her by, and she opened her eyes doubly wide to make certain I noticed before she turned away. I folded myself into the nearest couch, a shining thing of red-and-gold stripes. Procula came bubbling in my direction.

"Joanna," she said, "my dear friend."

I smiled, straining to understand my hostess, who delivered every sentence with trills and coos. "I've been waiting for you." She stretched out her hands but quickly drew them back in a strange half greeting. I had long since learned to accept such behavior without reacting. There are people who refuse to be in the same room with any who have suffered from consumption. Some doctors won't treat us for fear they will fall ill.

"Tell me everything," she urged me. "I've been waiting."

My face burst into a moist heat. "There is nothing to tell you, really," I began, dabbing my throat with a handkerchief. My illness sometimes filled me with flashes of inner fire that caused this embarrassing wet condition.

The whole room seemed to be watching us. Some of the devout women among us had probably been there at the women's court and witnessed my humiliating departure. Procula was the only one bold enough to ask.

"I wish I had the pluck to do what you did this morning," she said, delighted with me. "I'm always trying to find ways to attract handsome men. To have Manaen rescue me! What was it like?"

"I don't know how to describe it," I said. My hostess was a woman who fed on gossip and scandal. I was not about to offer myself as her next meal.

"Don't be shy," she coaxed. "My astrologer already told me." Her eyes grew as wide as orbs. "His Magnificence, Lord Darius, predicted it. A woman from the north, someone I knew, would come to Jerusalem. And a god would abduct her." In her excitement she spoke faster. "When I heard about your adventure at the Jewish temple, I knew you had to be the one."

"No, it wasn't like that," I answered, trying to quiet her. "I may have heard a voice, that was all."

"Of course you did," she interrupted. "Dear Joanna. The God of the Jews is very powerful. What did he say? He must have told you something."

Silent and smiling, I looked at her but did not reply. At last she seemed to understand that I was not going to say any more about it. Blinking her eyes, she reached for a plate of spice cakes and sank her sharp little teeth into one. I must have let out a sigh as I settled into the couch.

She leaned toward me again. "I know you've been in frail health, Joanna. I hope you don't mind my saying so."

Her honesty did surprise me. No one mentions another's illness in public.

"I know a Greek in Jerusalem," she said. "He uses fish oil to treat all sorts of problems. It must taste dreadful, but I've seen results. I could introduce you."

"That is very kind." I did not want to offend her by refusing her twice in one afternoon.

"Apollo. Have you heard of him?" She lowered her thick, round eyelashes to suggest a secret. "I used to suffer terrible sleeplessness," she said. "He gave me this charm that I wear all the time." Opening the waistline of her dress, she showed me a glass vile filled with specks of what looked like bone, tied on a cord stretched tight around her waist.

I thought of Mary and how she promised to speak to her son for me. "There is a man in Galilee," I said. "He heals even incurable ailments. His mother is my cousin."

"Maybe I should meet him." Procula moved closer. For gossip's sake she was willing to compromise her safe distance.

"I haven't actually met him, myself," I said. "Not yet."

"What is his name?" She was sitting right beside me.

"Jesus."

She frowned. "I thought I knew everyone. I've never heard of him."

"He lives in Capernaum and keeps to the northern towns," I said. "He has been working miracles for some months. Crowds of people follow him, but he is not yet well known outside of Galilee. When the time comes I will tell you about him." It was presumptuous of me. Mary never said she would introduce me to her son, only that she would talk to him about me.

"I have always liked you," Procula said contentedly. "We are alike. You have, how shall I put it, an appreciation for the supernatural."

I smiled without answering.

"Perhaps when you are next in Jerusalem you will come to see me again." She did not press her offer, but courtesy required that I accept. Better a friend at court than an enemy.

Chuza came for me. He wanted to have another word with the governor on our way out. I waited with the servants, watching Pilate as he sat slumped in his sturdy chair. I could see even from a distance that his dark head was filled with as few engaging ideas as ever.

I supposed Chuza was telling him about the citrus harvest in Galilee. My husband and I were traveling back to Sepphoris the next morning, so that he could spend his days in the fields with the workers and his nights in his own bed.

I wrapped my cloak around my shoulders to hint that our visit might soon end, but Pilate was not ready to let us go. Like a wolf drooling over a snared bird, he motioned for Chuza to bring me to him. Poor Claudia Procula, I thought. How does she live with such an unappealing man?

Chuza gave me no warning as we approached the royal chair. Pilate hardly acknowledged me but spoke only to my husband, saying that he had met with Manaen that morning. Chuza nodded; not a ripple of concern crossed his face.

"He told me there had been a problem in the temple precinct, I'm sure you know," Pilate said, twisting his enormous face toward me. I smiled, perhaps too eagerly. Chuza lowered his eyes in my direction, a familiar gesture that silenced me.

"Oh, my dear, I hear you lost your way," Pilate said in pained sympathy. "Whatever were you doing at the temple? Your family gave all that up years ago."

"I had never seen the festival." In my fear of him, my voice faded to a whisper.

Pilate pressed a hairy ear in my direction.

"I only wanted to see," I spoke up. "I'm sorry if I upset anyone."

The governor rolled his thick head back toward Chuza. "Your wife shows unusual curiosity," he said. "I am curious about the Jews, myself. We should know our enemies. But not at the expense of safety."

"It won't happen again, Governor," Chuza said.

Pilate pressed my husband's shoulder to his own as a sign of confidence, but he did not look again in my direction.

The long ride to Sepphoris was made even longer because Chuza refused to speak to me. He got lost in his strategies for organizing the workers and counting the crops. I sat across from him, watching him grind his teeth, as if he were chewing on his plans. His distant manner distressed me. I straightened the petals on a gold collar I wore that day. It never hung right, even after three trips back to the jeweler.

"Manaen betrayed us," I blurted into the strained silence.

"He had to say something," Chuza answered without even looking up. "If Pilate found out another way, we would both be in trouble."

"I don't like him."

"Manaen is an honorable man."

"He could at least have warned you."

"He did, I saw him this afternoon."

"Why didn't you tell me?"

"You're better at acting sorry when you haven't rehearsed. I expected that Pilate would ask about the temple."

We fell back into our separate places and did not speak again until we were in Sepphoris. The house smelled of lemon leaves, reaching upward from their stone vases. Chuza breathed the comforting scent, and the persistent tic above his eye stopped twitching.

I was preparing to leave him after dinner when he did his best to make peace.

"Let's put it behind us," he said.

"I'm very sorry." It was a heartfelt apology and he knew it.

"It turned out all right."

"I didn't mean to cause you trouble."

"I know that," he assured me.

In the days that followed, I plunged into the care of the house, determined to please my husband. I had the servants scurrying until every bedcover and window drape was hoisted down and heaved onto the back terrace. Table linens, kitchen towels, camisoles, tunics, bed jackets, my husband's robes—all were heaped like a termites' nest of cotton, silk and linen.

It took several days to soak so much laundry in the two vast wooden barrels of hot water we prepared. Scrubbed and rinsed clean twice over, every washable item in the house got attention. The back courtyard resembled a fuller's workroom. Linens hung drying in the sun. I went barefoot the whole time, grateful for plain stone floors to walk upon after the excesses of palace living.

Our third evening in Sepphoris, my husband said he would spend the next night in the fields with the workers. He often did so during the harvest, to show the men that he was not above hard labor.

"I'd like to go to Nazareth," I said. "I met a woman from there. She is my cousin."

"You didn't mention her."

"It was before our trip to Jerusalem. Her name is Mary."

I described our family relations, hardly an unusual story. Judea, ruled for centuries by foreign invaders, had few unbroken households. Brothers had turned against one another. Sons had abandoned their fathers.

"You will be home by dusk," Chuza said. "We don't need any more excitement."

The next morning my carriage rattled over city streets, past the bridge where peddlers pushed their trinkets at me. Another time I would have been tempted by their bronze amulets that promised a cure for foot sores, toothache and sneezing fits. That morning I wanted only to see Mary.

Octavia fussed over my pillows and asked if I was warm enough until I eased her hands away and she settled in to her needlework, reinforcing the silver on one of my husband's evening cloaks.

The winding road to Nazareth was clear until we came upon workers repairing the aqueduct. They were finally getting around to it, after the Passover delays. Five men on a scaffold hoisted large rocks to replace those washed away by the rain.

Phineas slowed us to a crawl. He was always fascinated by the efficiency of so many ropes and pulleys, buckets and planks in motion. The workers' heavy bundles swayed and lurched.

Octavia let out a clucking sound of disapproval and looked at Phineas in the driver's seat just ahead of us, as if to suggest that I should signal him to hurry. I took up my writing tablet and made a note. *Butcher—cut of beef for ten.*

A muffled thud warned me. Turning toward the sound, I watched a huge rock break away from the crumbling arch and crash to the ground. Two men at the top of the scaffolding lost their balance and fell. I watched with open mouth as one landed on the iron gears that moved the pulley. He was spiked on the sharp gears. I leaned over the side of the carriage and threw up.

"Now we'll never get through," Octavia groaned. She had not seen the men fall, or my sudden illness.

"We've got to help them," I said, not certain what to do.

Octavia's expression told me she wondered whether she'd heard me correctly. I called to Phineas. He stopped the horses, climbed down from his place and soon stood beside me.

"Go and ask if we can do anything."

He looked at me twice to be certain that he understood. Unlike Octavia, he would never think of questioning a command. He returned to us, asking for bandages. Octavia handed him a box from under the seat.

I opened the latch and prepared to step down. "Are you sure?" she pleaded. My husband's warning came back to me. No more trouble. I closed the door and waited. Phineas returned once again. "One is dead," he reported. "The others should be all right."

The foreman rode toward us, waving us on. The purple stripe at the hem of his tunic explained his polite attentions. A higher-ranking man, with at least two stripes on his tunic, had sent him. Our escort led us past the accident, and we continued on our way. Octavia rolled her sewing project between her fingers, preparing some sort of speech.

"If I may say," she began.

I kept still, inviting more.

"It is dangerous for a woman to stop and help strangers." She was not correcting me so much as curious about my actions, it seemed.

"What if one of my servants had an accident on the road?" I asked. "Wouldn't you want someone to stop for him?"

"Did something happen to you at the temple in Jerusalem?" Octavia asked.

"No," I said.

Mary, my cousin, was the only one I would tell about my morning at the temple. Without her to explain it to me, I had no words for the mysterious encounter. Even though I did not yet know the meaning, I was certain of what I heard in the women's court. Bursting with excitement and gratitude, I wanted to do good for someone else. That is why I stopped for the laborers. But all of this was more than I could express to my maidservant. I looked out the window until she went back to her needlework.

From below the town, Nazareth's hillside of caves resembled a bee's comb. Some of the caves had shacks in front of them for extra living space. We moved slowly along the rugged switchback that had been pounded smooth by the goatherds.

The carriage was too wide to squeeze through the town's narrow lanes. Before we left it at the livery, I packed Phineas with sacks and jugs until he smelled of the barley, dried cod and palm oil he carried. Octavia placed a basket of apples over her shoulder. The villagers watched us with suspicion. We were strangers, not to be trusted.

I recognized Mary's compound by the sign above the gate. A carpenter's level announced the family business. We entered the courtyard. Phineas went to my cousin's door and knocked. She opened it so briskly that the air stirred around us. In quick steps she came outside and dusted flour from her dress, vigorous as a young woman. Her large scarf could not contain the thick dark strands that rolled across the edge of her forehead. I smelled spice cake.

"Joanna, come in," she said, opening her arms to me.

I followed her like a curious child.

She greeted my servants as if they, too, were guests. I took my place on the small couch built into the wall where she had motioned me to sit. They stood near the door. She offered me a cup of warm water flavored with citrus and honey, then she offered the same to my servants. I nodded at them to accept it, although I was as confused as they were by the offer. They drank quickly, not moving from their places. When they were finished, I sent them to the inn at the north edge of town to wait for me as we had planned.

Mary went to her worktable, a clutter made from clay bowls, a jug of oil, a sack of flour and small linen pouches filled with expensive spices. I wondered if they had been a gift to her. They were an extravagance in such a modest home.

She brought me a taste of one of her cakes and began to wrap the other in fig leaves. "My brother-in-law likes these," she said, as if I knew her family. I only knew that her husband was a carpenter and builder who had died not many years ago. And of course I knew of her extraordinary son.

I moved to a small wooden stool near her table. My warm drink soothed my rough throat. "My servants are not accustomed to being received like guests," I said, allowing a hint of confusion.

She went on sweeping the table with a small fir branch. "Once, we were slaves in Egypt," she said. "Now it is our turn to be good to strangers."

The scent of almond oil wafted from my hair, threatening to overpower us. When I lifted my hand to remove my costly gold earrings, my charm bracelet clanked like cowbells.

Mary paid no attention. She admired the full sack of barley and the clay jug. "You are very generous," she said.

"We have more than enough at home." Tears suddenly sprang to my eyes. "Plenty does not always bring peace," I burbled. The powerless feeling that illness brings came back to me.

Mary went on clearing the table in silence. When she spoke, it seemed at first that she had changed the subject. "My father owned orchards and wheat fields," she said. "He offered twenty sheep at the temple when I was born. But he only wanted sons, not a daughter. I know that the rich can also suffer."

I encouraged her, and listened as she told me about our younger years. I imagined the life we might have shared as cousins, if it had been allowed.

"My mother admired you," I said. "She told me how good you were to your parents when they were old. I wish I had known you then."

"When I was still young everything changed for my family," Mary said. "My father lost his land to Herod. We left Sepphoris for Nazareth and he seemed to age overnight."

"My father cut our family off from yours," I said. It troubled me, now that I understood it. "We followed the Roman powers and made enemies of our own relatives." A sense of loss had been building in me as I listened to Mary. I might have been raised as she was, according to the holy customs.

Mary's stories about her childhood filled me with fantasies about how I might have fit in. She was twelve years old when her family fled Sepphoris, and at the time I was three. Her father refused to live quietly under Roman domination. My father made friends with our conquerors and said that only rebellious Jews fought the Caesars' ways. He called them Jews, as the Romans did, not Hebrews as they call themselves. He avoided my eyes when he told me these things. I knew he felt shame.

My cousin placed her gift of a small cake into a basket and started for the door. "I want to deliver this while it is still warm," she said. In the open courtyard she was taller than I had noticed. Not taller, exactly. She moved with refinement, like a wellborn woman who is content among villagers.

Two little girls who sat in the sun twisting sheep hair into thread ran to Mary and pulled at her basket, eager to help her. She kissed them both and let them take it from her.

The courtyard was shaded by a battered tarp. Small houses lined the walls, each with a furnished room on the roof. As we crossed the open space, passed by the central fire pit and the small round oven beside it, a black-robed man came through the gate. Glancing toward him, Mary leaned down and straightened the girls' braided hair. "Take the basket to your grandfather," she said, pointing toward one of the larger houses on the courtyard where cactus grew in a patch of sand near the door.

Mary looked back at the man who had come into view, but she did not wait to greet him. I could see from his prayer shawl that he was a man of authority. An elder of the temple, I supposed.

"Tell me," Mary asked as we walked toward her door, "have you seen my son?"

"I came to ask you about him," I said. "I would like to talk to him."

She watched the ground as we went along, an amiable expression on her face.

"I told him about you," she said. "We might see him this afternoon. He sometimes comes home for the Sabbath."

We went inside, still ignoring the shrouded man who was coming in our direction. Mary began putting spices away on the shelf. I watched her from my child-size stool, imagining what I would do if the healer were to enter the room.

A swift knock at the door set my heart racing.

"A blessing on your house," a voice called. It was a deep, rich voice.

Mary went to meet her caller. He was oddly made, with short legs and a bloated chest like a crow. His tasseled robe raked the dirt floor.

He bowed to me as we were introduced. "Ephraim, son of Benjamin," Mary said. "This is my cousin, Joanna, daughter of Abijah." She offered him the place on the couch and filled his cup. He could barely hold it with his stubby fingers.

"I did not know you had a cousin in Herod Antipas's court." Ephraim forced a bitter grin.

"We were separated for many years," Mary said. "Time has brought us back together." She was careful with this man and answered in few words.

"Your son, Jesus. Is he well?" The deep voice oozed concern.

"I don't see him as often as I would like." Mary took dates from a covered jar and placed them in a bowl beside Ephraim.

"People tell me that he works miracles. Countless numbers of cripples follow him wherever he goes. Does this please his mother?"

"I pray that he will always do what is pleasing to his Maker," she said, alert to possible trouble, I thought. Ephraim nodded his approval.

"Our families have made offerings together at the temple from the time your father brought you and your mother to Nazareth," he said. His forehead was as smooth as an olive, the grooves of a farmer's face did not mark him. He was a man of learning.

"You honor me by coming to my house," Mary said. She was unwavering before him, yet not defiant.

"A woman who loses her husband needs someone to talk to," he said. "It is not always easy for her to understand the world."

"I am grateful for your offer." Ephraim turned his shoulder toward her, as if to exclude me.

"Your son," he said, pausing for an extra breath. "He even heals on the Sabbath."

"I have not seen this for myself."

"The law teaches us that the Sabbath is the day when we take no step toward work but only praise the Almighty."

Ephraim stood up and walked toward the door as he opened his arm to invite my cousin to approach him. He lowered his voice and turned his back to me. "I only ask out of concern for you," he said. "A good son guards his mother's reputation." I strained to hear and did manage, just barely.

"You taught my son from the time he was a boy," Mary said. "You know how he reveres the ancient faith."

Ephraim regarded her tightening lips and crinkling brow. It was a blatant evaluation that had the odd effect of settling my cousin. She became serene and confident. Ephraim nodded patiently, a father indulging a misguided child.

"Peace be upon your family," he said as he went out.

Through the open door, the first shadows of evening stretched across the room. Mary began to fill her table with fish, bread and a mash of herbs for the Sabbath meal. How often, I wondered, does someone like Ephraim come to question her about her son?

"Do you think Jesus is right to spend his time with the sick?" I asked. I was sick, after all. I was unclean by her people's standards. Perhaps she feared that I was possessed by a demon.

"I pray the Holy One will protect him."

The sound of the ram's horn announced the setting sun. I stood and wrapped my mantle around me. There was no time left for easy conversation.

"I heard a voice at the temple in Jerusalem," I said. "Do you believe that it could happen?"

"Tell me what you heard," she said. She stopped and listened carefully. Standing near her, I recounted all that I remembered. "If it was the God of the Hebrews, won't He speak to me again so that I can be sure?" I asked.

She looked at me directly and paused to be certain that now I was listening to her.

"Are you waiting for Him to call your name a second time, so that you can be sure?" she asked. "There have been others who have heard that call. And if they answered 'yes,' their life was never the same again."

A sudden chill ran across my arms. It was true, then. The God of Mary's ancestors, my ancestors, knew my name.

I began to fasten my brooch. She came closer to help me as my hands were fumbling. "I promised to be home," I said to disguise my haste. I had to be on my own, to try to understand my cousin's words.

"There will be other times," Mary said. "I am not sure that my son will be with us this evening."

"Do you think my life will be different now, because of what happened to me at the temple?" I asked.

"We will see," she said, embracing me before I left her. "Perhaps the Holy One has plans for you."

We were not far outside Nazareth when a cloud of dust in the road announced travelers coming in our direction. Phineas pulled over to let them pass by. A group of men rounded the curve.

Jesus was walking with them. I recognized him by his

height—he was taller than most of the others. His shoulders turned slightly inward, as if some part of him wished to be left alone.

He was still a distance from me when I whispered what I can only describe as a prayer. "Help me." The words came from deep within. There was no doubt in my mind that this man could heal me. He was filled with the power of God.

"Help me, please, I am ill."

He lifted his chin in a gesture that reminded me of his mother. He asked who had called to him. The others did not know.

"Man of God, heal me."

He turned, more certain now, and faced my direction. He raised two fingers over me and moved his lips. The surface of my chest began to buckle and wave like a sail picking up wind. My skin rippled. A great heat rushed through my chest and arms, through my fingers. I slumped over, certain that I was going to die.

Octavia ran from the carriage and soon returned, panting. "The healer says to take you home, you need rest," Octavia said. We passed him on the road as Phineas galloped the horses toward Sepphoris. I tried to call out to him, but I had no voice. I believe he understood me.

CHAPTER FIVE

Then Jesus told them a parable.

—*Luke* 18:1

I spent the night coughing and spitting. Drenched in my own juices, mumbling nonsense, I am certain I terrified the servants. Octavia rushed to her room, took the last of the cow's hair she'd been saving for emergencies and placed it at her shrine to Hera, begging the patroness of good wives to take care of me. Phineas rode to the citrus groves, found Chuza and brought him home.

Or, so I am told. From the time I left Nazareth, I was not entirely of this world. In my daze I crawled over rocks and tripped over scrub brush, running from a snake that coiled around my chest no matter how many times I tore it away.

Chuza was asleep in his tent when Phineas reached the

camp. My husband is slow to wake up and cannot manage to dress unless everything is in its place. His tunic was laid out for him near his couch, but he could not find the insignia for his belt. Phineas took the small night lamp from the top of a trunk and searched. A dull glimmer of bronze, nearly buried beneath dirty laundry, turned out to be the missing piece.

Chuza arrived at home that night to find me thrashing like a captured alligator. He took in the sight with an inspector's eyes. There was my nurse, dabbing my forehead with a cool cloth, as if I were fragile glass. My Roman doctors were unusually grim. The room was stifling. Someone had closed the windows to keep out bad air that might encourage my disease.

My husband approached my bed, nearly tripping on a large brass bowl half full of my brown spittle. No one thought to get it out of sight before he arrived.

All of this led him to conclude that I was dying. He started bossing the servants, to help him forget his worries. One of them opened the window. Another placed a chair close to my bed so that Chuza could sit beside me. He shooed away the nurse once he saw that he could dab my hot cheeks at least as well as she did. His touch, heavy and familiar, told me he wanted everything back to normal, immediately. I could not speak, or I would have reassured him that despite what he saw, I was improving.

The doctor offered his bleak report of the night's events. My husband made no reply, which can be more frightening than when he roars. The poor doctor pushed a speculum into my throat, trying to seem efficient. He extracted a sticky blob, heated it over a low flame, winced and shook his head to say there was no change.

He could not have guessed what was taking place inside me. I could feel my illness rising up one last time like a chicken that has lost its head to the ax but hasn't yet given up the fight. My husband's halting breath against my throat told me he was terrified. I heard him order Phineas to go and find Jesus. I was certain I must have imagined it.

Chuza did not believe in miracles. Long before I met him, he gave up all hope of divine intervention. His wife-beating father had convinced him there was no help beyond human effort. Eventually his anger toward heaven turned to indifference. Religion became like a foreign language.

In the last moments of my delirium, it felt to me as if a fire's embers warmed the room. Opening my eyes, I saw Jesus. Servants and the doctor cleared a path for him. Chuza moved closer to me, a cautious protector.

Jesus entered with steps so light I could not hear them. He reached for my hands and spoke my name. "Joanna," he said. "What has happened?"

"I am improving since I last saw you, my lord," I said.

It was not only that I felt stronger. For the first time in my life I had some idea of what it meant that there is a God, one who watches over us with love and compassion. I knew that was why a great healer had come into my life. God sent Jesus to me.

He did not inspect the staff as Chuza had, but asked my husband to send everyone away. Jesus leaned over my bed and placed three of his fingers above my lips, feeling my light breath. He bent lower and covered my mouth with his. Chuza was about to pull him off but stopped and let his hands drop to his sides. He was powerless to help me. He had to allow Jesus his chance.

At first, I too was afraid. No doctor had ever placed his mouth over mine in that manner. I did not resist as he gently blew his breath into me, filling my lungs the way a fresh breeze fills a rustling curtain. My chest began to rise and fall on his strength. We continued this way for some time. I closed my eyes and saw a fountain of light flowing through me. It was clean and refreshing.

I only looked up because Jesus stepped back from me. He watched to see what would happen when I tried breathing on my own. Gurgling sounds came out of me. I felt my insides change, from soaking wet to drier. I heard the steady rhythm of normal breath and it was my own.

My husband fell to his knees beside my bed. He studied my face for a long moment, then dropped his head against my drenched nightdress. The weight would have been un-bearable in my previous state. But I was healed.

By now it was early morning. I looked at my visitor. His face was paler than when he had first entered our house. Chuza crossed the room at great speed and threw open the door. "Bring us something to eat," he ordered. Hurrying back, he spoke to Jesus for the first time. His voice wavered with emotion, but he fought back his feelings as well as he could.

"Thank you," he said. "My wife is, she appears to be, recovering. Please, sir, tell me what I am to make of this."

"Why do you ask me?" Jesus replied.

"Are you a magician?" Chuza pressed him.

"Magicians only fool the eye," Jesus said. "Their sorcery does not last." He was a patient teacher. "All that I do comes from the Almighty One, whose works are true." Jesus settled his gaze on Chuza's face, baked brown by the sun. My husband's eyes grew heavy with tears. I could almost hear him commanding the drops to turn back. By habit, they obeyed him.

"Your wife is healed," Jesus said. "She needs clean clothes and something to eat."

The servants entered with plates of white fish, warm bread, figs and bowls of curds. I devoured my food like an athlete after a race. Chuza sat back and watched in amazement as I finished one course after another. Then he threw back his head and laughed.

Jesus ate, too, and drank my warm barley broth. My husband talked nervously about the harvest that was coming in ahead of schedule and the warm nights that allowed his men to work longer hours.

Somehow I managed to squeeze in a sentence. "Jesus's mother, Mary, told me to trust her son," I said. "And look. I was dead. Now I am alive."

"I hope it is over," Chuza said. His feeble smile said he was not convinced. It was the best he could do. "How do I thank you?" he asked Jesus. "You can have anything of mine that you want."

Jesus raised his shoulders, just slightly, as if there were no answer.

"I would like to do something," Chuza said.

"Remember what you saw here today," Jesus said. "Your Heavenly Father loves His daughter, Joanna. As much as He loves you."

Chuza nodded politely. Standing up, he knocked the table off balance. Backing away, he said he would call Phineas to escort Jesus back to his mother's house in Nazareth.

When we were alone, I reached for Jesus's hands. "I wish I could go with you," I said. I would have left everything behind. I can be impulsive at times.

When I was perfectly still, he answered. "Your place is here. Give thanks to your Heavenly Father. Take care of your husband and be good to those who live in this house."

Chuza returned with Phineas. Jesus refused the offer of an escort, preferring to walk alone. I supposed it was the only time he would have to himself that day.

When he was gone, I called for my husband and sent the servants away. He sat at the edge of my bed. I wanted to say that he must forget the pain of his younger years. I wished that he could, without my having to ask him.

"Are you well, my husband?" I began.

"I will be all right," he said. "I hope that you will be, as well."

"I am healed," I said, and placed my hand on his. "God sent Jesus to help us, Chuza. You will see. Everything will be different now."

"I want to believe you," he said. His shy smile told me he struggled with his doubts and did not want to spoil my happiness.

I could see the young man in him, the son who took care of his brother and his mother, the honorable boy who stood up to his brutal father. Chuza could not forgive heaven for what had happened in his father's house.

"Did you ask the gods to help your mother?" I seldom dared to broach the subject.

Chuza smoothed the top of his hair. "One night I heard her screaming and ran to her," he said, in an even voice. "I tried to pull my father away from her, but he threw me off. I rushed outside and shouted for Mars the warrior to save us. From next door my mother's brother and his sons came stumbling out of their house, half-asleep. By then my mother's jaw was turning black. She was never able to close her mouth properly after that."

I started to say that perhaps his uncle was sent to him at heaven's urging. The Holy One, who spoke to me, must have heard the call of a good young man hoping to save his mother.

"That was only one night," he said. "How can I believe in any god? They all turn their back on injustice."

"If only you would try once more," I said. "It will mean so much to me."

"Joanna, you are asking me to do what I cannot do." My husband's voice was a gruff whisper. I could see that I had offended him.

"It's all right," I said. "Maybe when you know for certain that I am healed."

* * *

Chuza was not at home on the day I opened our house in Sepphoris to Jesus and his friends. It was for the best. My husband was more realistic than I about the people who follow a wonder-worker. Thrill-seekers, pickpockets, troublemakers, he warned me.

Chuza had posted six extra guards on the grounds to help keep order, and arranged to spend the afternoon out of the house. The grape harvest was nearly finished, and he chose that day to review the numbers.

I had not seen Jesus since my healing and wondered if he would notice how I had changed. Some days I felt like a visitor to my own life. I was beginning to notice things I had overlooked—the way a camel stands up on its hind legs first, or the way a beekeeper hums when he goes near a hive. It felt as if the Creator of all life had arranged these small delights just for me.

My newly found love for the commonplace did not prepare me for the crowds that pushed through my gate and scrambled over my wall looking for Jesus. Before Strabo, my chief gardener, and his assistants had finished trimming my overgrown hedge, or the tent makers hoisted the tarps, the followers of Jesus flooded my property. The peacocks in the courtyard screeched and ran for cover. I wanted to do the same.

They came from every sort of background. Some were dressed in fine woolen robes and thick leather belts. Others wore filthy straw sacks. I passed through the yard, listening to the sound of the merchants speaking their coarse Greek, herders jawing in thick Aramaic. Some of the Hebrews murmured only in their own language, to keep outsiders at a distance.

I circled back to the terrace and greeted newcomers, keeping an eye on the servants I had stationed near the gate to greet our arriving guests. No matter how many I sent to help, they could not keep up with the crowds. One man passed them by altogether in a way that concerned me. His face was hidden beneath a large shawl and his hands were buried in his pockets.

I caught the attention of a guard who stopped him. I was soon informed that the man's name was Joseph, a spice dealer from Arimathea and a member of the Hebrew Council. We were introduced, I bowed lower than usual. It was not every day that a successful merchant and a religious man came to my home.

He presented me with a small purple linen pouch. I recognized it immediately. It was exactly like those I first saw in my cousin Mary's kitchen. I looked at him more carefully. His round, polished face was filled with laughter and gaiety. He obviously had a barber tend daily to his perfectly trimmed beard.

As I opened the pouch, it released the dusty scent of cinnamon. "From Babylon," he said. He had a supply of new spices with him and was on his way to sell them in Jerusalem. He had stopped in Capernaum on his way south to Jerusalem, when his friend Jesus invited him to my house.

"How do you know Jesus?" I asked.

"He sometimes rides with my caravan," Joseph said. "I go through his city in my travels."

"And you must know his mother." I held the linen spice pouch up, to suggest I had seen others like it at Mary's house.

"An excellent woman," he said. His round black eyes rolled like olives on a plate.

"I expect her to be here today." I watched for his reaction.

"Yes," he answered, as if he expected the same. So then, he did know her more than in passing.

I admired his fine woolen stole.

"I hope I did not upset you, entering your house as I did," he said. "At times I hide my face. It's only because I don't like to argue."

"Argue?" I asked, not certain what he meant.

"Some of my acquaintances want to question everything Jesus says. They dispute whether his teachings agree with the Talmud. I never know how to answer them."

He mistook my silence for a hint that I knew more than I was saying.

"Tell me," he asked, "what do *you* think? Could Jesus really be the one sent to redeem the Hebrew people?"

"I don't know," I answered. "He saved my life and I am forever in his debt."

Smiling happily, as if my small-minded answer was enough for him, Joseph excused himself. Could this man be my cousin's suitor? Could it be, I wondered, that her late husband, Joseph the carpenter, had somehow arranged for this successor to take care of her in his place? I took it as a sign that the carpenter was still watching out for Mary from beyond the grave.

The afternoon wore on. I made the acquaintance of a penitent wearing rocks around his neck, a woman covered with tattoos, a mute who responded to every comment with a raucous sound from his cymbals. With every new introduction, I grew more discouraged. This was the company my healer kept. How was I to fit in among his followers?

When a swine herder marched toward me, dragging a pig on a rope, I recognized his choppy accent. He was a Gadarene.

"This is for Jesus," he said, trying to hand me the rope. Phineas was one step behind him. "Tell your teacher he ruined my town." I had heard curses thrown down in a friendlier voice.

I was further informed that the sow before me was the only one left after Jesus passed through Gadara some weeks ago. He drove demons out of a possessed man and they had entered the herder's pigs, the Gadarene told me. Why else would the animals have run for miles into the sea where they drown?

"Here," the man growled, throwing down the rope. "Tell your miracle worker his friends the demons forgot one."

Phineas took the man by the arm and led him back toward the gate. I sent for my head servant and told him to pay a generous price for the pig and destroy it. There was something unlucky about the beast.

On the terrace, a small number of clean, well-dressed men and women seemed to be enjoying the happy sound of the drums. They were a pleasure to behold—if only there had been more like them.

Too many guests were closer in type to the Samaritan woman who walked into my garden and stormed past Joseph as well as several temple elders. They turned to avoid the sight of her plunging neckline.

I watched her go to the fire pit and rip a slab of goat from the spit. One of the cooks threw himself between her and the meat. "We are not ready," he said, more courteously than I would have. She ignored him and reached for more. I whirled around, looking for a guard. Instead, I saw my cousin Mary.

"Joanna," she said. At the sound of her voice my fingers relaxed. They had tightened into fists.

"My son is close behind me," she said. Her face glistened in the afternoon heat. Dust from the road clung to her sandals and the hem of her robe. I wished I had sent an escort rather than allow her to walk from Nazareth. I embraced her.

"Jesus healed me," I whispered. "I am not the same."

"I can see you are strong." With the sun on her face, she looked to be full of light. I saw it then. She was the one who had first asked her son, on my behalf. Jesus came to my sick bed out of love for her.

A waiter passed by, carrying a tray of pomegranate juice. I took a cup for my cousin and one for myself. The Samaritan woman ran toward us and dropped to the ground before Mary.

"Mother of the healer!" she shrieked. "Your son cured my daughter. She was like a wild dog. I had to chain her to a wall and often came home to find dark lumps on her head. Jesus wasn't afraid. He put his hands on her."

My cousin pressed the sobbing woman's shoulders against her round hips the way a mother comforts her child. Mary did not seem disturbed by the woman's tears but held her until she grew calm. When the woman finally stood up, she gripped Mary's hands for a long time. Then she drifted back into the crowd.

"Doesn't it frighten you when strangers throw themselves at you?" I asked.

"I understand the woman," Mary said. Her voice was full of kindness. "I am a mother, too."

"Did your mother worry about *you?*" I was always trying to find out more about my cousin.

"Good woman," a robust voice called from behind me. "I have been waiting to see you." It was Joseph, the spice merchant. He bent low, smiling at Mary with reticence and a hint of longing. I put my hand over my lips to hide my smile.

Mary stepped into the shade beneath a tarp and I followed. We sat on bright silk pillows and took in the view of the dense green valley. Joseph waited politely until we were settled. He then explained his plan to pass through Nazareth in two days' time. My cousin assured him that he was welcome. That seemed to satisfy him. Bowing once again, he left us.

I instructed a servant to go inside and close the shutters on my husband's windows. The sun was growing stronger. I reminded my cousin that we had been talking about her life as a young girl. Indulging me, she continued.

"In Nazareth, my father and mother depended on me to take care of the house. I was proud when I finally learned to balance a jug on my head all the way to the well."

She was back in her girlhood for just a moment, with her young friends. "We used to cover our hands with our sleeves." She demonstrated. "Smooth hands please a husband, we would say. None of us really knew. We were children."

When my father heard about Mary's engagement to the carpenter, he said that her father, Joachim, allowed it to shame our family. My father had cut every tie with Joachim, but he still considered Mary's marriage to a laborer an embarrassment. He was not a man of property.

"And so you married the carpenter," I encouraged her.

"Good afternoon." A deep voice interrupted. Manaen was standing close to our tarp. I wished he would leave us alone but greeted him courteously for my husband's sake.

"Good afternoon." I tried to sound welcoming. "May I introduce you to my cousin, Mary of Nazareth? Cousin, this is Herod Antipas's captain of the guard, Manaen."

He warmed to her gracious smile. I raised an eyebrow to suggest that he be brief.

Mary turned her inviting eyes toward Manaen, and to my surprise I saw a hint of recognition.

"Perhaps you have met," I suggested.

"No," Manaen answered. "We've never been introduced." Then, to my cousin, he said, "I have seen you with your son, in Capernaum. I sometimes pass that way." He pressed his hand against his upper lip to catch the drops of sweat.

"Come into the shade," Mary said, making room for him.

Manaen stepped under the tarp.

"What brings you here?" I asked.

"I have a note from the chief steward."

He handed it to me. I opened and read:

I will not be able to return home as early as I expected.
Manaen will help manage the crowds.

"I have heard your son when he is teaching in the fields,"
Manaen was telling my cousin.

"People come far out of their way," Mary said.

I was going to point out that Manaen rarely had reason to
be in Capernaum. It occurred to me, quite unexpectedly, why
he would go there. He was watching Jesus, probably report-
ing back to Antipas. Manaen was like a son to the tetrarch. Of
course he would advise Antipas about so popular a man of the
people as Jesus. And of course Antipas would feel threatened.

Mary looked from one to the other of us. "One day God
will bring peace to our land," she said. "My son and I wait
for that day."

For a devout Hebrew, peace meant the end of foreign
rulers. Manaen studied Mary's calm face but said nothing.

The jingle of tambourines coming from the terrace
signaled me that Jesus had entered my gate. We hurried
toward him. He was already locked in the crowd and could
not move or take a step unless everyone moved with him.
Several of his companions stayed close to him, trying to
soften the crush of people. He stopped for many who pulled
on his cloak or fell down at his feet. He gave his attention to
each one as if no one else mattered for that moment.

His mother kissed her son's cheek and stood quietly beside him. "They will be listening to everything you say," she reminded him. An elder of the synagogue at Sepphoris was close enough to hear her. Another one like Ephraim, I supposed. No doubt he would soon be knocking at her door to complain about her son.

"Don't be concerned," my healer said softly. Mary nodded her head just enough to show that she trusted him.

I went to the servants and instructed them to uncover the tables. The pewter trays of lamb and goat, baskets of bread and crockery filled with preserved figs pleased me. I stood on tiptoe to rearrange the grape leaves surrounding my apple cakes, and told the waiters to make sure everyone's glass was full.

We prepared plates for my healer and his mother. After they had been served, I stood back and let loose the hungry hordes.

Food and drink turned strangers into friends. I noticed Joseph, the spice dealer, stopping to admire my cousin, who sat with the other women. It was only a brief exchange, but her eyes met his. I wished I could read her expression more clearly, but her glance was mild and enigmatic.

Jesus moved from circle to circle. Before long he took off his sandals and stretched out on the ground as if he were at home.

"Master, tell us a story," someone called out when the servants were clearing away the empty plates.

For a moment Jesus looked over my garden. His eyes settled on Strabo, who was sitting in front of him. "In summer, when the flowers are blooming," Jesus began, "the gardener sees the fruits of his labor." Strabo put his arm around his little boy. He already liked this story.

"By then he has worked for long months, clearing away old leaves, cutting back the underbrush, turning the soil and planting new seeds.

"In the Garden of Paradise," Jesus said, "our ancestors did not need to work for their food." The crowd turned silent. "But I say to you, the new Eden is within you. What you sow and nurture now will lead to the harvest. Some of you will reap more bountifully than a rich man has ever dreamed of."

Strabo stood up and raised his arms toward Jesus, as if to say he was honored by the story. Reaching out like a man offering a gift, my chief gardener began to dance. One foot crossed behind the other. He stepped to one side and back again. Soon others joined him. The drums and tambourines picked up the rhythm. Slow at first, then faster. Two of the musicians leaped from the terrace and danced through the crowd, encouraging us all to move our feet.

We women formed our own circle. Soon we were a sea of dancing waves. I had never been strong enough to dance like that before, not since I was a child. I took spins and dips, amazed by my own vigor.

The men coaxed Jesus into their circle. Manaen linked arms with him, stepping and turning beside him with impressive skill. He had not been far from Jesus the entire day. I questioned his motives.

The scent of my garden, the jasmine, myrtle and rose, wafted through the air. Paradise could not be more fragrant. It had taken years of patient work to bring it this far. I tried to picture the neglected Eden inside of me and wondered how long it would take to make it bloom.

CHAPTER SIX

Now Herod the ruler heard about all that had taken place…and he tried to see him.

—*Luke 9:7, 9*

Chuza and I returned to the city of Tiberias in late summer. The erratic weather suited my mood. That time of year by the sea, the sun can be a sullen recluse one day, a raging tyrant the next. Desert winds are strong enough to knock the statue of Venus down from her throne at the amphitheater. It was under these conditions that Lucius Vitellius, a favorite of Caesar, paid a visit to Antipas's court.

Vitellius and Chuza both had served in the Roman Army. Military service seems to bind men together. When Tiberius Caesar inherited the throne from Augustus, he favored Vitellius, who was now on his way to being named governor of my husband's native Syria. A choice position—my husband's native land was still one of the most important of Rome's eastern territories.

Chuza and Vitellius got along well. Unfortunately, our distinguished visitor did not take as kindly to Antipas. I expect it was the way Antipas shamelessly flattered our guest. It was such an obvious attempt to gain favor.

For Antipas to rebuild Sepphoris in a style that rivaled the best Roman cities had made a bad impression on Caesar's competitive men. He went too far when he immediately built a whole new capital and then named it after Tiberius Caesar.

His grab for recognition did have one positive effect. It allowed Chuza to stay away from the new capital for a good portion of each year. Through the planting season and again at the harvest, he had to be in the fields near our home in Sepphoris.

Each time we returned to Tiberias, I wept. Cyclops-size buildings and garish statues crowded the streets. Antipas's villa lolled on the edge of a hillside, lending an air of danger. There was no telling when a rainstorm would wash the whole thing into the gully. He considered his house a showplace. Like the palace, the baths and amphitheater, his home was a reproduction of Roman splendor.

With his usual bad luck, Antipas built his new capital under a curse. The Greeks and Romans blamed Pan, the goat-legged meddler who lurked in the hills above the city. People lived in fear of his nasty humor.

The Hebrews hated Tiberias for their own reasons. It was built on land that had been an ancestral graveyard. Antipas's Roman-style city stood on the ancestors' bones. Hebrew religious teaching said that Tiberias was polluted.

The evening that my husband and I returned to the city, a bad taste settled on my tongue. In such a foul place there was no telling what would become of my newfound faith. I needed constant retraining, or I was doomed to fall back on familiar ways. Giving up bad habits has never been my strength.

After so many months away, oily vapors hung in every room of our cottage. They had wafted up from the hot springs at the bottom of our hill and slid freely through our shuttered windows while we were away. Their medicinal stink clotted the air. I burned cedar chips to mask the odor.

I had given the house a Roman flavor, to show my husband's support for Antipas. I went so far as to lure Nicolas, the most highly prized wall painter in Rome. He made the trip east only after I promised to introduce him to Pilate's wife, Procula, in Jerusalem. He had decorated every house worth mentioning in Pompeii before he ventured to my remote corner of the Empire. He considered it a step down, to work in the provinces.

The golden line drawings he placed against wine-colored walls in my dining room were some of the most elegant I had ever seen. I took pleasure walking past them again on our first night back in Tiberias.

Antipas sent word that he would dine alone with Lucius Vitellius that evening. We met them the next day at the amphitheater, slipping into our places just before the festivities began.

As the priestess bowed her way past the statues of the Caesars above the entrance to the theater, I knelt with the others, seized by a pang of shame. What would my cousin say if she could see me, bowing down to a stone?

The procession approached the statue of Venus, where the priestess draped a garland over the stone goddess. I felt like a liar. I had donated laurel from my garden for the occasion. I vowed never to do so again. A contented smile spread across my lips. It was the first since our return to the capital.

For so many years I had been the most fickle devotee of the Roman gods. I both called upon Venus and doubted her existence. She never seemed to answer my pleas. I looked up at her image, towering over the stage.

Devout Hebrews would condemn me for entering a place where Venus was said to reside. But my cousin Mary seldom saw things the way others did. There was room for questioning, at least. I resolved to spend more time with her. She would show me how to live according to her ways, and to be a true follower of her son.

Vitellius sank into his chair, bored. Chuza spoke to him, hoping to distract him. They picked up a conversation they must have started at another time.

"I'd like to see the new operations you were telling me about," Vitellius said.

"They've worked out well," Chuza answered. "The farmers resent them, of course. They've had to come in from the fields and learn new skills."

"It's better than starving."

"They'll never forgive Caesar for taking their land."

"They're difficult people."

Neither one mentioned that the Romans had forced the farmers to work as carpenters and foundry workers, after a lifetime in the fields. They talked as if it were all the same, whether planting or forging iron wheels for a living.

Vitellius asked about a pottery concern in Magdala known for a black ware with a provincial charm. The rustic style of it had caught on among the upper classes, and it had become a popular export.

"Antipas gets the credit," my husband said. It wasn't deserved, but no one in the tetrarch's court would consider saying otherwise.

"Yes, of course," Vitellius agreed. Conversation threatened to collapse.

"Have you seen the actor, Paris?" I asked. "I understand he is one of Caesar's favorites. We only managed to have him here for you because Herod Antipas arranged it."

"I never much cared for theater."

A dwarf with an enormous head waddled onto the stage and announced the play. *Scenes from the Lives of the Gods*. They were inescapable.

The sun was now directly overhead. I wished Antipas had planned it so the jugglers and ropewalkers had opened the show. It was difficult to concentrate on a play with the afternoon heat at its most demanding.

The audience cheered as Paris walked onto the stage, in the role of Athena. He had perfected the feminine postures of the Greek goddess as she whittled a flute of her own design.

When she finished carving, she blew into the instrument and made beautiful sounds, but she happened to catch sight of herself in the reflecting pool. Drawing back, she faced us with her bloated cheeks and squinting eyes before she tossed the flute aside if it were her enemy. How could anyone take this goddess seriously? She was as vain as I was.

One story from the afternoon's performance did impress me. When Paris, playing the nymph Daphne, ran away from lusty Apollo, she rushed fleet-footed across the stage and back again. Each time she crossed before us, she was covered with more leaves and strips of bark. She was turning into a tree.

At last she stopped at the center of the stage, extending her neck and arms into graceful branches. This was always my favorite of Ovid's stories. Now, suddenly, it seemed more believable than before. I touched my feet and ankles, half expecting to feel the rough skin of a tree. As the nymph Daphne began a new life that was different from what she had ever known, I knew that I was like her.

I could hear the tetrarch whining as our Roman guest shuffled to his feet. "Paris expects us in his dressing rooms after the performance," Antipas insisted. No use, Vitellius was preparing to leave. "It's too hot out here," he said.

Our entire party stood with him. There were ten of us in the tetrarch's box. The audience craned to see what was the matter. Soon, no one was watching the play.

Herodias ran to Vitellius and fanned his neck in the most inappropriate way. She had no sense of propriety. He climbed the steps toward the exit. Antipas motioned for the audience to sit down and sent word to the stage that the play should continue. "Stay until the end, keep the crowds calm." His hand gripped Chuza's arm as he spoke. His best efforts at impressing his guest had failed, yet he still managed to conduct himself like a ruler in complete control. Waving at the crowds as if they adored him, Antipas hurried after Vitellius.

By evening our guest from Rome was well enough rested to attend a dinner for Paris. Antipas cornered him at one end of the room. I was seated with the women as usual, but ignored their talk and listened to the captivating Paris, whose thin voice carried well.

I could hear Chuza's voice, bass notes in a trio, reviewing the afternoon's gladiator games with anyone who would listen. They had been the final event of our day. Thankfully, I missed most of the bloodletting. My eyes were squeezed shut. The crash of clubs against breastplates was all I could be sure of.

The next morning, Chuza and I sailed from Tiberias to Magdala with Caesar's counselor, our weary visitor from the west. We docked and went directly to the pottery workshop. I was invited because I was expected to choose gifts for Vitellius to bring back to Rome. Outside the workshop two boys walked back and forth, shouting at passersby.

"Miracle pitchers. Pitchers, inside."

I was not fully awake and did not pay attention.

We entered a clean work space of stucco and tile. Six potters were at their wheels and several others crushed black stone to powder that was used to color the clay.

The manager walked us through the rooms, boasting of organized schedules and increasing demands for his wares. He rushed us into the shop next door. Shelves of identical black pitchers covered one wall. Taking one down, smiling to expose the holes where his teeth once had been, he pushed the good-size vessel toward us.

"This is what you're looking for," he said. "The miracle pitcher."

"Miracle," Vitellius repeated dully.

"From the wedding party last spring." The shop owner's voice grew loud enough to attract anyone who might be walking by, outside. "A servant filled a pitcher just like this with water." With his grand gesture, our attention was drawn to the display shelf.

"This servant hurried to his master. By the time he got there the water had turned into wine."

"That can't be." Vitellius had no patience for this story. He started for the door. Chuza followed.

"It was a mother's persistence," the shop owner called after them.

"A mother?" I asked.

Chuza was immediately at my side, instructing me while barely moving his lips. "Find something for the counselor's wife and hurry. We'll wait outside." Looking over the shop with a proprietor's pride, my husband went to find Vitellius.

"Mary, the mother of a great prophet from Nazareth," the shop owner answered me. He went on to tell of a wedding in Cana where his niece got married. Her family owned a collection of Magdala pottery, gifts from the shop owner through the years.

"The Nazarene prophet was at the wedding with his mother," he explained. "I was dancing right near him when she came looking for him. There wasn't enough wine left for the fathers of the newlyweds to drink a toast."

By now I was clutching a pitcher. "The prophet's mother told her son. The host would have been shamed," the shop owner continued. "Pretty soon a pitcher just like this one, filled with water, was pouring out wine."

There are people who make an art of caring for others. I was starting to notice that my cousin Mary was one of those people. It wasn't only me she looked after, much as I would have liked to think so.

Chuza's heavy footsteps sounded near the door.

"Give me three of your most popular serving bowls," I demanded. Then, under my breath, "And one pitcher."

"We are ready," I said. My husband was watching, impatiently.

On our return to Tiberias I was escorted home without my husband. That evening when Chuza came in he went directly to his rooms. I finished my copy of a drawing by Nicolas that I had been working on and went in to say good-night.

"Vitellius seems to be in good health," I said.

"I suppose." Chuza was at his desk, surrounded by record books.

"I trust your meetings were of interest?"

"Somewhat."

"Only a few more days and he will go on to Syria."

"Yes."

I went closer, hoping for a better view of Chuza's face. "Is everything all right, my dearest?"

He put down his work but did not look at me.

"Caesar has heard complaints about Antipas," he said. "Vitellius asked me what I knew."

The worst of it, Chuza explained, had to do with a prisoner Antipas executed some months ago. He claimed the man was plotting against the government and had him beheaded without a hearing.

"Vitellius tells me the man was not a rebel at all," Chuza said. "He worked for Caesar. He was an agent."

This agent had been sent to Tiberias to investigate reports that Antipas was collecting taxes from the Hebrews that never reached Rome. The agent must have found some proof.

"Vitellius will report whatever he learns while he is here," Chuza said. "It will make things difficult for all of us."

Chuza's restless feet shuffled under his desk. I felt sure that he knew more, possibly worse, than he was telling me.

Two days later, typical of life at court, the official farewell for our Roman guest was more than polite. Afterward, Chuza walked toward the tetrarch's chambers with him. I walked behind them with the women.

I did not expect Antipas to speak to me, although I knew he must have heard about my healing.

"Joanna," he said, waving me forward. "I hear you've been cured."

"While we were in Sepphoris," I said.

"Some miracle worker from Galilee, wasn't it?"

"Yes." It seemed best to say as little as possible.

"You don't even look like your old self." I touched my neck. The scarf I usually wore to protect against the open air was noticeably missing.

"It is true, I am healed," I replied.

"Do not forget your loyalties," he said. His thin lips curled into a sneer, their most comfortable position. "There is only one man in Galilee who rivals the greatness of the gods," he said. "And that man is me."

"Of course."

"Remind me, what is the name of your healer?"

I told him.

"Oh, yes, Jesus," he said with a smirk. "I think you should spend more time with your healer, Joanna. Get to know him better. Then come and tell me all about him. I would like to meet this wonder-worker of yours."

"But my husband." I pointed vaguely toward Chuza, only a few steps behind us, to suggest that he wouldn't approve.

"Oh, come now, Joanna. Surely you can think of some way."

Chuza and I walked home from the palace. I could feel him sifting through the events of recent days.

"Chuza," I said when we stopped to rest near the willow trees. He had been well ahead of me, not one to enjoy leisurely walking.

"Yes," he answered without any impatience.

"Herod Antipas asked me about my healing."

"Has it been that long since we last saw Antipas?"

"He said he wants to know more about Jesus."

"What does that mean?"

"He says I should spend more time with him, and tell Antipas all about him." Chuza was already shaking his head disagreeably.

"If he wants to know more, he can go to Capernaum himself."

It was a ridiculous suggestion. We walked on in silence. I was out of breath as soon as we began to climb the steep hill that led to our house. At the sound of my panting, Chuza stopped.

"We're going too fast," I said, hugging my sides. "Can't you slow down?"

He was sorry, he'd forgotten. Not everyone had the strength of an ox. He took a flask from his belt and offered me a sip.

"What did you tell Antipas?"

"I said I didn't think you would approve."

"Joanna," Chuza said. "Can't you see how many things can go wrong?"

"Would it really matter if I spent one day in Capernaum?"

We walked on. He stayed ahead of me. I whispered a request, one of my increasingly more common attempts at a prayer. "Please, show us the way."

Two brown thrushes hurried past, flying close to each other and then veering apart. The male soared higher, the female dipped low. They must be newlyweds, I told myself. Still learning to bend their wills for the sake of the other.

We scaled the last slope to our cottage. I held my hand over my nose as we passed the mineral baths. Chuza waited for me at the top of the hill.

"All right, then," he said. "Spend a day in Capernaum. And let that be the end of it."

He must have known, as I did, that a day would *not* be the end of it.

CHAPTER SEVEN

Someone told him, "Your mother and brothers are standing outside, waiting to see you."

—*Luke* 8:20

The smell of perch grew stronger as we neared the shore at Capernaum. Glistening lights in the sand proved to be fish scales tossed there by fishermen cleaning their catch. As we drifted toward the jetty, I wondered out loud whether the house where Jesus stayed was close to shore.

"It's on the other side of the city," Octavia said. It was beyond her to keep still if she knew an answer. What she lacked in discretion she made up for in useful information.

We climbed the steep path leading up to the city, past fields so recently harvested they still smelled of onions. As we entered, the townspeople stared at us, but I hardly paid attention. Hebrews and others lived peacefully in Capernaun—I had no reason to expect trouble. When a young man's shrill voice ripped the air, I did not even suspect that he was shouting at me.

"You were choking to death on your own blood," he taunted. "Your Roman doctors couldn't save you." His leather apron was streaked with soot. A blacksmith's chisel dangled from his pocket. "People like you are ruining Capernaum!" he shouted. "Go back where you came from. Leave us alone."

I was not about to let him run me out of the city where my healer lived. "I was sick and dying," I answered. It was completely unlike me to speak to a crowd of strangers, but I had to defend myself. "I asked Jesus to help me, just as many of you have done. I owe him my life, just like many of you."

Phineas did not wait for a response but moved us through the city gate. We stopped only to ask directions at the wood-carver's booth. He put aside a small statue of Astarte, the fertility goddess he was carving, and pointed us beyond the center of town. We were to look for the house with the black kettle hanging outside the door. The woman there sold fish stew at dinnertime. She could show us where to find Jesus.

It was rare for me to pass by an idol-maker's booth without buying a carving to place inside my sleeve for protection. The carver must have sensed my interest. He came out from behind his bench.

"Let me show you," he said. I don't know why I followed him around to the back.

"The goddess is here, in a secret place. You will see."

He opened a curtain at the back of his booth. A billow of incense smoke rolled from behind it. I went inside, trying to see through the clouds. I stepped up to an altar with a shallow brass bowl on it. Smoke rolled out from the bowl. I was curious.

The carver held out his hand to show me a mound of tiny wood-carved infants. He quickly held his hand over the fire and dropped the babies into the embers.

"This will please Astarte," he breathed, worshipfully watching the statue of the mother goddess. "She takes all lost infants to herself and sends healthy new babies in their place, if a mother prays for such help."

I could feel droplets rolling down my face. I stumbled backward.

"Chuza," I wailed. Twice, our babies had died inside me. I thought my husband would never stop grieving the loss of them. All the illness in the world could not excuse me. I lost my husband's sons.

It was a memory I had buried and left behind. Now it raked across my heart once again.

Octavia's arms were around my waist. She led me away from the altar and hurried us onward. I could hardly walk. She pulled me along. We came to the city square, and Phineas led us to a bench in the shade.

It was unnaturally quiet. No one sat under the linden trees or stopped at the baker's stand. It was as if people had dropped what they were doing and gone running after something, or someone. A small army of scorpions had the place to themselves. They had piled up on a baby lizard when the poor thing was not yet dead. Its tiny legs wobbled helplessly in the air.

Phineas got us moving after only a brief rest. He kept turning around, looking to both sides, sensing, as we all did, that something was not right. I almost said we should turn back, but by then we were outside the house with the kettle at the door. Phineas knocked. An old woman opened, scowled at me and began to shut us out.

"Is this the house where Jesus of Nazareth stays?" Phineas asked.

She opened, just barely. "He isn't here," she said.

"Can you tell us where to find him?"

She opened a bit wider, cupped her hand over her eyes to shade them from the sun and pointed toward the courtyard door.

"Go back," she said. "Pass two more doors on the right and enter the third. He is there." She was gone before we could thank her.

The scent of dry mud walls filled my nose as we walked down an alley so narrow I could touch the compounds on either side. Sheep pens cluttered the way. We squeezed past them and went on.

At the third door we entered a small compound with a staircase at one side to suggest that there were eight separate dwellings. We moved into the crowd and made our way toward the house at the far corner.

Tapping on shoulders, speaking into strangers' ears, Phineas coaxed people out of our way until at last we reached the house. I followed him inside, with Octavia close behind me. Sorting through the crowd, my eyes finally settled on Jesus, sitting on a chair in the center. The noise from the courtyard made it difficult to hear.

"Master," someone said. "You cure our sick, and I myself have seen you feed as many people as fill this room although you had hardly any bread. Some people say you are Elijah."

The heat of the room dampened his face. Tiny swirls of dark hair lay matted against his ears. When he spoke, he was fully a teacher, challenging us to follow his argument. "Do you believe in me because I cure you when you are sick?" he asked.

A blush of shame came over me. I felt as if he was asking me the question. I was not sure of the answer.

"If angels descended from heaven and attended to me," he said, "then, would you know who I am?"

Two men pushed their way toward the door. "He thinks he is some kind of prophet," one grumbled.

A young boy swished past me and surfaced just ahead, bobbing above the crowd. "Master," he called. "Your mother and brothers are outside."

Jesus looked at the boy.

"They want to speak to you," the boy said. Some of the eagerness had fallen out of his voice.

"My mother and brothers." The words drifted to the floor.

There was murmuring, a few more people started for the door. "He's out of his mind," someone scowled.

There was shuffling and the sound of feet stepping aside. A man in a brown striped turban passed by. I stepped out from behind Phineas for a better view.

Jesus spoke the man's name, Simon. I glanced over my shoulder at Octavia. "Broth-er" she mouthed.

Simon leaned toward Jesus, trying to speak privately.

"...a fool of yourself" is all I heard.

The room was so still that the squeal of a pulley at the well on the hillside seemed very near. I pictured the old woman with the kettle at her door, drawing water for her fish stew. Another shuffling of feet was followed by loud whispers. I turned to see my cousin Mary entering the room. She walked with certainty and a slight suggestion of a smile on her lips. Jesus stood up to greet her.

"Why have you come?" he asked, polite but not inviting.

My cousin looked at the faces closest to her in the crowd. No one made any effort to give her room.

"We have expected you at home," she said.

"This is my home," Jesus said. "Here is my family."

His eyes were shining like those of a man who has not slept in days. "Come home and rest," Mary said. It was more than a suggestion, but not a command.

Simon spun around and started clapping his hands at us like a herder chasing strays.

"Clear the room," he said. "Please, leave us alone."

He stretched out his arms to sweep us toward the door. I took baby steps and went sideways as often as forward. Every time I looked back at my cousin, she was speaking intently or waiting expectantly for Jesus to reply. I heard only parts of their conversation.

"How can you say that?" she asked him. At the end of another long sentence, she added with some emphasis, "Even in Nazareth." My healer opened his lips to answer her, but she went on, determined he would hear her out.

I must have lost track of what was happening around me. Suddenly my feet left the floor and someone's arm was around my waist. Straining to see who dared to touch me, my cheek brushed Simon's beard. Phineas grabbed the man's throat and tightened until I felt myself being dropped to the ground.

My servant would have killed the man if I had not stopped him. The three of us stood like confused cattle. My cousin came to Simon and gripped his arm with her broad hand.

"I wish I had never met him." Simon twisted his face toward the front of the room.

"F-forgive me," I stammered. "I should have gone out with the others."

Simon bowed with a hint of apology and walked toward the front of the room.

"Come with me," Mary said. If I hoped for an explanation about what had just passed between her and her sons, I was disappointed. "There is work to do before the evening meal."

We went through the courtyard into the street. My cousin led the way back to the house with the kettle and entered alone, then returned for me. I sent Phineas and Octavia back to the boat for the blankets and the lamps I brought from home as gifts. I followed my cousin through the kitchen of the house to an outdoor terrace where whitefish dried in the sun. The old woman dozed near the wall.

"This is Hannah, the wife of Nathan," my cousin said. "She has been very kind to my son." The old woman got up and put me to work mashing olives and herbs into a paste and grinding wheat on a stone so basic it lacked a handle. My arms ached, but I did not allow even one sigh. I consoled myself by imagining I was planting seeds in my own private Eden.

My cousin and I cleaned the fish and stripped the kernels from their cobs, then carried everything to the fire and assembled a stew exactly as we had been instructed. I stood back from the heat and watched Mary.

"Do you come to Capernaum often?" I asked.

"Not so often."

"But you hear stories about your son."

"Sometimes, yes."

"A mother still worries about her son even after he is grown," I suggested. She quietly plucked fish bones from the broth with her fingers. Then she came and sat beside me on the large flat stones.

"I worry that he is not safe," she said.

"But the crowds revere him. Who would dare to harm him?"

"You saw it—he offends people with what he says, comparing himself to prophets. It is too much for them."

"But you?" I ventured. "You believe that he is a great prophet, and more than that, don't you." I immediately wished I had not asked. If she doubted him, what was I to believe?

"I am sure of this," she said. "The Lord who gives us life does not want to see my son chained in prison." For his own protection my cousin would not defend her son's pronouncements that he was the Messiah. Not even to me.

I left her alone and went to find us some water. It was blistering hot. When I returned, the strained expression around her eyes had softened. "Once when he was a little boy, he ran outdoors at night," she said. "It was close to the festival of Succouth. We had built a booth in the field near the house. It fascinated him. I thought he was going outside to admire it in the moonlight.

"I followed him so that he would not wander away. When I reached him he was standing on the wall, watching the sky. He seemed to be listening to something that I could not hear. I called him. He answered me like a sleepwalker, not fully awake.

"He said that he was going to be greater than all the prophets, one day. He spoke the words as if he were repeating a message he had received. I did not ask him to explain but held him close, to calm my own fears."

My cousin's story disturbed me. I rose to my feet, took a few small branches from the woodpile and fed the low fire.

"You worry that what he says to the crowds could make trouble for him," I suggested carefully.

"When he lived at home, I could watch out for him," my cousin answered. "Now it is not the same."

"I will send my best servants to guard him," I said. "I will give him anything he needs. Money, food, a horse and cart to take him through the towns."

Mary moved the cooking pot away from the heat.

"He has to live his own way."

"I can give him anything he wants," I said.

"All he wants is for us to trust that God will take care of him."

The old woman, Hannah, called us back to the house. "Hurry," she said. "They are here."

I spent most of that evening in the kitchen, helping to serve the friends of Jesus. There were twenty or more of them, all reaching across the table, dribbling food into their beards, wiping their fingers on their clothes.

I stayed busy cleaning up after them and then I ate, standing, in the kitchen. At the end of the meal my cousin filled a bowl with apples and almonds. "Bring this to the table and take your place," she said.

I went out and would have sat near the teacher, but a boy who was beside him moved closer and left no room for me.

"Chuza," I sighed, just under my breath. It was always clear with my husband what was expected of me. I was the wife of Herod's steward. We were the most important family in the territory, after the tetrarch.

In this house, I was not sure. All of us were strangers, trying to get along despite our differences. I swore I would not come back to Capernaum.

Jesus told us that we should take care of one another. I looked around the room and tried to imagine it. Fishermen, farmers, widows, barren women—these were his closest companions. Yet I resolved that I would help his followers in any way that I could. Another tiny seed planted, in my long-neglected Eden.

Octavia and Phineas spent the evening stealing glances at me. I was, after all, being treated as a servant. Phineas barely ate his food or moved from the place where he stood near the door. He was a watchman by nature. Octavia chattered with the women who sat near her on the floor. I could hear her, asking them about everyone in the room.

Well before sunset my cousin went to her son and told him that I was returning to Tiberias. We were about to leave the house when Hannah came to me.

"Find them safe houses where they can stay in their travels," she said, smiling at me for the first time. She had thought of something useful for me to do.

"I will try," I said, imagining myself trying to explain to Chuza.

We all stood up at once, and several of the people in the room came to walk with us back to the shore. As we went through the city, our small group grew larger. Neighbors came out of their houses and followed us. Joseph, the spice dealer, joined us along the way. I did not notice him until he was embracing my healer. He must have arrived in Capernaum at that hour.

It was not long before he worked his way closer to my cousin Mary.

"Blessings upon you, good woman," he said.

She welcomed him with her eyes, although she was discreet. An unmistakable air of contentment settled over her.

I heard him say, "I will bring them to Nazareth."

"Two cows?" she asked, amused by his promise. "You are bringing me two cows?"

"I hope I do not offend you," he said, reticent all of a sudden.

My cousin quickly understood that he was, indeed, serious. "They will be a luxury for my family," Mary assured him.

I let them go on ahead of me and I walked in the sweet scent of their affection. My cousin's romance only added to the mystery of her. I could never fully solve it, which made her all the more irresistible.

We started down the hill toward the shore. A man near the beach waved his arms toward us and called out.

"I have news from Tiberias," he said. I felt a knot tighten in my stomach. He ran up the hill toward us. When he reached us, Jesus was about to grasp his arm, but the man pulled back. Like a wild animal, he shunned human touch.

"The Baptizer is in prison," he said. "He waited for Herod Antipas outside the counsel meeting, and accused him in public."

The men swarmed around this new visitor with a face like cracked leather and hair that looked like a thornbush. The Baptizer, I was informed by the other women, was named John. He lived in the desert with a group of men like the one standing before us, withdrawn from the world that was corrupt beyond recovery.

The wild man shouted his story at us. "John stopped Herod Antipas in the street in Tiberias and condemned him in public

for breaking the law," he said. I had to ask again for explana-
tions. I was informed that Hebrew law forbids a man from
marrying his brother's wife unless she is a widow. But
Antipas's offense was worse than that. Herodias was his niece.

It was beginning to make more sense. John the Baptizer
had insulted Herod Antipas by accusing him. He had humiliated Herodias. My throat turned dry. I could not speak.

People started giving me orders. I was to arrange for the
Baptizer's release from prison. I promised in a froglike croak
to ask my husband if he could help. Immediately I wished I
had not said anything.

When we were in the boat, pushing off for the open water,
I stared back at the shore, trying to hold on to the peace that
filled me when my healer blessed me before I left him.

I went to Capernaum only to offer my assistance in a
general way and to see for myself what my healer's life was
like. I came away with impossible tasks to achieve, and I had
seen more than I cared to in Capernaum. My cousin Mary
could not reassure me about her son. She was struggling to
understand him, herself.

The rippling waves turned from orange to black in the
sunset. I lost myself in my problems. Where would I find
anyone willing to help me with my new task? Who could
I ask to open their house to the rough-edged followers I
met in Capernaum?

As the amphitheater at Tiberias came into view, I tried to
imagine how I would talk to Chuza about releasing the
Baptizer from prison.

I closed my eyes and only opened them because I sensed someone near. Octavia was sitting beside me.

"What did you hear from the others?" I asked.

Her ramblings about the best silk vendor in Capernaum, the upcoming fishermen's competition and other news of the city amused me. She could be such good company, my Octavia. She helped me forget my own silent turmoil.

CHAPTER EIGHT

Go tell that fox for me...

—Luke 13:32

Chuza was waiting for me on the dock at Tiberias. I could see him standing with his arms roped across his chest, his expanded chest. Sometimes, to seem more imposing, my husband squared his shoulders and pulled himself up to his fullest height. It added a bit to his stature, but I could still see over the top of his head with no trouble.

The servants lit the lamps as I walked past them toward my husband. My bright smile announced that I had kept my promise and returned home before dark. The natural crease near Chuza's lips was unusually pronounced. I could tell that he had made up his mind about something and I should proceed with caution.

Rather than tighten my own considerable jaw in reply, I felt a rush of gratitude for him. My husband was a good man who tried his best to please me. I pressed my cheek against his smooth, warm face. My nearness eased his tight manner, but he did not return my embrace. Chuza loathed public shows of affection.

We rode home along the waterfront and were about to climb the final hill when we came upon Manaen near the mineral baths. I could not see him from my litter but heard Chuza say the name as he slowed his horse. I put my ear against the curtains and listened.

They spoke of some dull accounting matter, but then my husband mentioned that I was just returning from Capernaum. Manaen lowered his voice and suggested that he would like to hear more about my trip, sometime. I sensed a double motive. Sitting up, twisting the gold band on my finger back and forth, I fought an urge to open the curtains and demand that Manaen explain himself. He was even bold enough to suggest that he escort me on my next visit. Chuza put an end to the conversation with his curt reply. "She isn't going back," he said.

Storm warnings blustered around my husband that evening as he moved restlessly through the house. He didn't ask about my day. Out of politeness he did raise a few bland questions that I answered politely.

Yes, I said, I was treated well in Capernaum. My day there had been enjoyable. Indeed, I assured him, I found my healer without any problem. And, just as my husband had predicted, the breeze was with us as we sailed.

We managed a peaceful evening, except for one brief squall. "Do you know of a preacher named John, a baptizer?" I asked, on my way to bed.

Chuza recognized the name right away.

"His friends are worried about him," I said, perhaps with more urgency than was wise.

"They shouldn't be," Chuza growled. "He's in prison, but he hasn't been condemned."

"Do you think you might help him?" I asked.

The deep line near Chuza's lips tightened again. "The man is no concern of yours." He finished by adding, "At the next Jewish festival, the crowds will demand his release. That's how these things are handled. You keep out of it."

My husband was clever to remind me of the custom. Antipas released a prisoner on the major feast days. I smiled vaguely to show that I was content, but I wasn't, not entirely. It was some consolation to know that the Hebrews' Festival of Lights was close.

Late that night, Chuza came to my room. I was jotting a few household notes on my tablet. Halfway to my bed he paused and smiled a bit shyly. His voice was inviting. He said he had been surprised how much he missed me during the day. My husband had not spoken to me in that way for many years. I put aside my notes. He said I was more beautiful than he had ever seen me. My cheeks and figure had grown appealingly full and round.

I rose and took a step toward him. He reached for me. His hard, narrow lips against the curve of my neck awakened old feelings. Chuza had not touched me with such heat in his hands since I lost our sons.

After years kept apart by illness and worry, my husband had returned to my bed.

Before dawn's light I felt the regular breathing of Chuza's deep sleep. As a new wife it had disappointed me when he dozed too soon in the night. Just as I was about to profess my deepest feelings, his tensed thighs would fall like lead against me. But that night, I smoothed his dark boar's hair, moved my hands over his iron shoulders and wrapped my arms around him to keep him safe. Chuza was the one treasure I could not replace.

The next day I followed behind Strabo in the garden as he cut back the rosebushes before the cold weather, and shouted at him when he pruned too much. Poor man, I hovered each time he pulled up a weed, to be sure it wasn't a delicate wildflower worth saving. He knew more about the garden than I ever will, but fussing over him gave me a sense of purpose.

In the garden I could sort out my thoughts. The rich, freshly turned dirt, the bright faces of the moistened leaves reassured me. A natural order ruled in my garden. Perhaps that same divine power guided my own life.

My husband was home before dark. I offered him the juniper drink he liked so well, but he had no time for it. He slowed his course long enough to slide his hand along the outline of my arm on his way to his rooms. I had not yet managed to tell him about the promises I made in Capernaum. It was starting to wear on me.

Before dinner I instructed the servants to leave us alone once the tables were in place and our couches were arranged near the pecan trees. They were among my newer possessions. Since I'd met Joseph, the spice dealer, I had called on him several times to ask that he bring me seeds and saplings.

How discreet he was, never to let on that he cared so much for my cousin. For once, I'd found something out for myself. Octavia had not helped me.

Chuza came out to the garden, wearing a cloak and all of his courtly gold, dressed for Antipas's birthday party. Only the men of the court and the officers were invited. I accepted his quick peck on my cheek but clung to his hand, slowing him down.

"Will you talk to Antipas about the Baptizer?" I asked.

"I'll see," Chuza answered. There was the deep crevice, again, etched in his jaw. It was his way of saying no.

My husband returned home very late and pounded up the stairs past my door to his own rooms, then came back to mine. His face was pale and shining. I thought he had been drinking too much, which would not be like him. He never let down his guard when he was at court. He glared, his expression shifting from anger to fear.

"The Baptizer is dead."

I pulled the blanket tighter around me.

"Antipas had him executed. His head was the final course. On a platter." Chuza's shoulders began to shake from an unnatural laughter.

My husband was no stranger to killing. As a young soldier he would break a man's neck between his hands. At the arena, I never saw him turn away when wild tigers ripped apart the prisoners in the ring. He had a huge tolerance for violence, as any man in Antipas's court had to.

"Herodias was behind it," he said.

I was about to ask, when I remembered the wild man's story. The Baptizer had shamed her by accusing her husband.

Chuza held his hands toward me as if they were a scale, with one object on each plate. "The baptizer and the miracle worker," he repeated, weighing one against the other until his hands slowly struck a balance. The hair on my arms lifted and fell in a wave.

"One of them is now dead."

"What do you mean?"

My husband collapsed against my door, still holding the imaginary weights in his hands.

"Chuza, you're frightening me."

He looked at his hands, curious over what he found there. "Joanna," he said. He was trying to fit my name into his terrifying equation.

I went to reassure him, but he pressed his arms against his chest and would not let me near him. "No," he shouted. "Stay away."

He pointed one thick finger at my face. "I forbid you," he said. "I forbid Capernaum."

He left me then, stamping down the hall to his rooms. Dazed, I listened to him slam cupboards and drop heavy objects to the floor. He paced, sat down, paced again. There was no sleep in the man.

The next morning he was gone before I rose. I remembered that he had a meeting with gold merchants from Corinth, negotiating tariffs.

When it was still dark I called Octavia. I told her about John's beheading.

"Find out whatever you can about the circumstances of his death," I said.

Her feathery eyebrows rose in a double arch.

"Does the healer know?"

"Yes," I said. It was never a good idea, with Octavia, to let on that I did not have an answer.

"Go to the market. Listen, and be careful."

She returned by midmorning.

"John's followers were outside the palace," she said. "Some of them started throwing rocks at the gates. Soldiers charged into the crowd."

I stood from my couch and went to the window. There was no one on the road. It was eerily quiet. Our gates and gardens were undisturbed.

"What are people saying about his death?" I asked.

"Herodias ordered it. She wanted revenge."

"The woman is dangerous," I said. "I wouldn't trust her with my closest friend."

I looked at Octavia. She was my servant but also my closest friend.

My husband did not return home for two days. He arrived in the afternoon, protected by armed guards. The city was under curfew. A number of rebels were in jail. Antipas was furious about the uprising. As far as he could see, it was never his fault when there was trouble.

Chuza and I went to our separate rooms, he to pace and bump into furniture for another night. I prepared myself to tell him about some of the things that worried me.

The next evening we stayed at home. Before retiring, I went to Chuza's rooms. "You were right," I said. "I didn't want to see it. Capernaum is too dangerous. I swear to you, Chuza, I will not ask again." I could not bring myself to say out loud what we both knew. It was not safe for Chuza that I should follow a close friend of the Baptizer.

My husband was red-eyed and exhausted. He seemed more willing to talk than he had been in some time.

"Antipas let John's followers take the body," he said. "That satisfied them."

"What will happen?"

"We'll go back to normal."

From that day and for many to follow, my husband was consumed by his work. I stayed out of his way and spent afternoons in my rooms with Octavia. I was completely unsettled, as he was, and tried to keep busy. I made lists of friends I might trust enough to ask a favor. Could they make a place for Jesus and his disciples, when he passed their way?

Octavia tried to help by suggesting names. But she objected to all mine and I rejected hers. I was left with a list of three. My gardener, Strabo, had a brother living in the Decapolis who worked for me when I needed extra hands. There was Octavia's aunt, the wife of a stonemason in Caesarea Philippi. A third possibility, less promising, was the sister of my aged cook, Bernice. My kindly servant had been with me from the time I married. I knew she had a sister, an eccentric goatherder living alone in the hills above Nain. Bernice always spoke of her as a generous woman. I prepared a basket for the goatherder.

None of my three choices had the slightest interest in pleasing either Roman or Hebrew authorities. All of them were good people from what I knew of them. And they could all use the money.

Each afternoon Octavia and I worked in the kitchen with Bernice. She was nearly blind, but well able to work with her hands because she was so familiar with the ways of the kitchen.

We wrapped salted fish, palm oil and jars of honey for a messenger to deliver, along with my request for lodging. One day, as the sea breezes rustled clean linens drying in the courtyard, Octavia glanced at me, then at Bernice, to suggest that she wanted to talk to me, alone. I excused my half-blind servant.

Bernice had barely shuffled out of the room when Octavia started in. "We all sat in the same room, in Capernaum," she said. I could not argue. All of us, wherever we may have come from, had crowded into the same room to be near Jesus.

"I found it uncomfortable," I said offhandedly, distracted by my task.

"The women were together, with the men," she persisted. "Slaves and their mistresses, together. You and I both worked in the kitchen."

"As we do here," I offered, not sure of her meaning. "I wish some fathers treated their own children as well as the least among us were treated in Capernaum. Look at you—your father sold you as a slave, but he spared your older sister." Octavia frowned to warn me that I had completely missed her point.

"All of us ate from the same table," she said.

"That was odd," I agreed, certain that she found it unnatural.

"The Master said that is how it should be," she corrected me.

I stopped what I was doing. My maidservant had been confused. I understood how it could happen, but felt I had to clarify the facts for her.

"We all have our place in this world," I began. "That is what Jesus told me, in this very house, the night he healed me."

Octavia's sallow skin turned blotchy, but she did not answer me.

"He told me to take care of those in my household," I said. "I am responsible for you."

She played with the packing straw on the table.

"I am asking you," she said, "for my freedom."

My hands dropped to my sides, as if they belonged to the dead. The flutter in my chest convinced me I was on the verge of a coughing fit. I answered her in what came out as a tiny voice.

"Are you unhappy here, Octavia?"

"I was not born to be a slave."

"But we are almost like sisters," I said. "I have given you everything. Is this how you would repay me?"

"Nothing is more valuable to me than my freedom." She showed no gratitude. I might as well have treated her like a doorstop all these years.

"I cannot discuss this," I said. "Not now."

Octavia turned sullen. We fell back into silence.

When law and order had been restored in the city and the curfew was finally lifted, I received an invitation from the tetrarch's palace. The golden scarab imprinted on it belonged to Herodias.

"The ladies of the court," it read, "a private viewing...a new acquisition," and so on. "Five in the afternoon," the day was noted. Her quarters, there would be no escaping it. Chuza knew nothing about it when I asked him.

"She wants to show the women her new pet," I said. "I can just hear her." I imitated her guttural accent, "Ladies, pleeeze. My pan-ther was cap-churet for me een Eendia."

"Careful," Chuza said.

"You can kees his nose, eef you like."

My husband wagged his head to disapprove of my performance.

I dressed simply that afternoon to avoid outdoing my hostess, which would be difficult. Her tattooed ankles and hennaed palms were beyond my limits. And her hair—far be it from me to advise her against wearing it as she did. It hung over her forehead like a black curtain, in the style of Cleopatra.

Servants and valets fell over one another to receive us at the palace. I passed through Herodias's new garden. Cactus, shaped like men's body parts. It had been long, happy months since I last saw Herodias's apartment with its marble-pebbled walls and red swags at the doorways.

Unsuspecting, I paused at a wall painting near a purple couch. It took me a moment to recognize the scene. A band of straggle-haired nymphs skulked through the woods under the morning stars. Coming upon a camp of men who lay asleep on the ground, they tiptoed closer.

From there, I had to look more carefully to be sure of what I was seeing. Tormentors, they preyed on the unsuspecting men for their own amusement.

I drew back, as stunned by the lewd scene as if I had come upon it in real life.

Herodias kept us waiting and entered with servants trailing behind her. Four of them carried a large, dome-shaped object covered by a black sheet that they placed on a table near the center of the room. We moved closer as she motioned us to toward her. Herodias was not good at public speeches. I plastered a smile on my lips.

"Ladies, hear me," she began, waving us in. "I have something you will want to see."

Her voice was a thick gurgle. I held my smile despite her long, awkward pause.

"That is so," she continued, pointing toward the mystery cargo. "I have wanted to own this prize." Another strained pause, then she turned and snapped her fingers at a servant, who stepped forward and lifted the veil. She folded her hands across the huge lapis belt buckle on her stomach.

I saw a box made of iron that resembled a latticed prison door. Herodias unhooked a latch.

"Can everyone see?" she asked. "Ladies, look here, please." The door swung open. I was close to it and had a clear view. A human head hung inside the box, the tongue thrusting from a gaping mouth.

I dropped my cup. It rolled noisily on the floor. A din followed as more cups slipped from frightened hands. Gasps and shrill giggles bounced around the room. Some of the women from the back moved to the front. I stepped aside, feeling dizzy enough to faint.

A guard came in, carrying a pole with a sharpened edge. A few, precise thrusts and he spiked the head, drew it from the box and handed it to Herodias. She was gleeful, hoisting it up like a warrior with the enemy's remains.

A servant near her took hold of the pole to steady it. Herodias pulled the knife from the servant's belt and gouged out one eye from the Baptizer's wounded face. She screamed in delight, baring her horse teeth.

"Everyone, follow me!" she shouted. Dancers suddenly came from nowhere and musicians stepped in behind them, parading around the room. The moment Herodias turned her back to me, I rushed through the door, fanning myself before the servants as if to say the excitement was too much.

I hurried along the colonnade, following the sound of tinkling water until I reached a courtyard. My eyes were all but closed as I went. The bloodied head, the broken teeth, the jagged flesh torn by the ax. I had never seen the man, in life. Gagging, I leaned against a pillar and stood motionless. It was some time before I felt able to go back.

Returning the way I came, I passed several rooms I had not noticed. As I crossed in front of one I heard the unmistakable sound of Antipas's voice.

"Joanna," he called.

I stopped, not even sure where the voice came from.

"Here," he said. "I'm right here." I entered a wide double door, into a blue room where dolphins swam in a wall mural. It was like being underwater.

"Jo-an-na," Antipas cooed as I approached his chair.

He pointed to a seat near his, but lower to the ground. I sat, looking up at him.

"Well, then," he said. "So much has happened."

"I hope you are well, Herod Antipas," I said, smiling like a happy idiot.

"And you have been to Capernaum, where your healer lives."

I stretched out my answer, hoping to keep from saying too much. "Yes, yes I have."

"Tell me about him, Jesus," Antipas said. "They call him the rabbi, don't they?"

"He is very kind," I said. "The people rush to see him."

"What does he say about me?"

"You? I haven't heard him say anything about Herod Antipas."

"Good, I like him better already."

"He talks about how to live well."

"And what does he say about that?" An oiled marble floor was no more slippery than Antipas.

"He says heaven is inside each of us. We can make our life here seem more like paradise, by our good works."

"You say 'we,' Joanna. Am I to take it that you have become one of these... Jesus people?"

"Well," I said, trying to hide my mistake, "well, all of us are free to follow his teachings."

Antipas's sinister chuckle set my lips trembling. I looked at his pointed chin, his small, close-set eyes. Fox was the right animal. They all called him that behind his back.

"Joanna and the Jesus people," he said. A twitch in his eye set the lid fluttering. "The crowds adore him. And he baptizes them. He's like the other one, the one whose head now belongs to my wife." He stopped and seemed to be listening again to his own cleverness. "Of course," he said, curling the words around his lips. "Jesus is the Baptizer, brought back to life."

I could not get up from my chair. I felt like a stone figure held forever in carved granite. There was no escape. Beside me sat a man who was tumbling down to the edge of madness.

"Joanna," Antipas said. "I'd like to meet this teacher of yours. I want to listen to him. You arrange it." The sparks in his eyes warned of a dangerous fire.

"But he travels with the caravans," I resisted. "He can't leave his work in Capernaum. People go to him if they want to see him. He spends all his time with the sick." I tried everything I could of think of.

"Calm yourself, Joanna," Antipas said in a mocking tone. "I don't have to meet Jesus right away. As soon as you can, arrange it."

"My husband has told me I am not to go back to Capernaum," I said. "My place is here, at court."

"Your husband is a shrewd man," Antipas smiled. "But your tetrarch says that you can go back. Or, send word and tell your healer that Herod Antipas wants to meet him. I leave the details to you."

He stood up and thrust out his hand. I kissed his ring, looking briefly into his eyes. There it was again, the lunatic's glint.

I spent the rest of that day hiding in my rooms, listening for my husband to come home. Octavia drew a warm bath, which did not calm me. I said nothing to my maidservant. We were hardly speaking to each other, which made it easier.

At last Chuza came walking along the portico. My mirror told me that my afternoon spent bathing, resting, curling my hair did help to disguise my ill humor. I sat near the window that overlooked the garden. Ripe pomegranates burst open on their branches, jewel boxes dropping rubies. Such beauty was some consolation.

"My husband," I said, reaching for Chuza and smiling at him. I felt stronger, just to have him near. He was not as agitated as he had been during the long days that followed

Antipas's bloody birthday party. I pressed myself against his chest. Without questioning me, he held me quietly.

We finally spoke, in low voices. I told him about my terrifying day at the palace, repeating every exchange I could remember. He let me speak, asked no questions, said only that Antipas had seemed to be in good spirits during the counsel meeting, earlier in the day.

"I would like to send Phineas to Jesus," I said. "To ask the Master if he would agree to go to the palace and meet Antipas. I would arrange safe lodgings for him."

Chuza considered my suggestion for some time, before he corrected me.

"Not Phineas," he said. "Manaen."

"Manaen?" I must have gasped. "Why Manaen? Phineas knows where to find Jesus."

"Manaen will convince the rabbi that he will be safe here."

I placed my fingers against my forehead, trying to press out the knots beneath my skin. There was no point in arguing. Chuza sent a messenger requesting that Manaen come to the house the next morning.

The leather-bound hero arrived promptly. He looked at me with his liquid green eyes. I thought I saw a hint of admiration. I parried, trying to read his true motives.

I served him raisin cake and oranges. Manaen was, after all, my husband's friend. Chuza allowed me to be in the room when he explained his request. He sounded as if he were describing a mission.

"The tetrarch has asked to meet my wife's healer," he began. Manaen's eyes wandered. Something was making him feel uneasy.

"Are you going to pass near Capernaum soon?" It happened that Manaen was going to meet a delivery of copper coming from the north. The caravan was due in Capernaum within a few days.

Chuza did not go into details. It was apparent how they worked together, speaking in unfinished sentences.

"I can stop on the way," Manaen said.

"My wife knows the house where Jesus lives," Chuza said.

"I think I know," Manaen said.

"Do you?" I asked. He had more than a passing knowledge, it seemed to me.

"I'm sure I can find it," he corrected himself.

I described the house, watching for further signs that he already knew the way. It was obvious that he knew more than he let on about Jesus.

"What am I to tell him?" Manaen asked.

"Please tell him that the tetrarch is curious to listen to the teacher," I answered. "Say that Joanna, the wife of Chuza, will arrange for his travel by boat. Tell him, this is very important, that I myself will find him safe lodging while he is here."

All that day I prayed that Manaen would return quickly and bring my healer. I added something to my prayer that I had never attempted. I fasted. I ate and drank nothing. I thought of it as one more little improvement in my newly reclaimed garden, a secret work in progress that came to mind every day, lately. It was some satisfaction to imagine a few more rocks and dead leaves cleared out of the way.

On the evening of the twelfth day, Manaen finally returned. He had been gone several days longer than I expected. But when I said as much to my husband, he suggested that the caravan may have been late, or the shipment may not have met standards. Chuza was not concerned about the delay.

Manaen came to see my husband at home, although he could have waited to see him alone. I was grateful for that courtesy—it allowed me to hear directly what he had discovered in Capernaum.

My husband received Manaen in the green room, which is small, easier to heat in winter and more private than the main rooms of the house. After a time Chuza sent for me. I noticed in Manaen's eyes a hint of sympathy as he looked at me.

"I found Jesus in Capernaum," he said. "And I explained the tetrarch's wish."

I smiled hopefully.

"He refused to come here."

My hand flew to my lips before I could stop it.

"His ancestors' bones are buried in the ground where Tiberias now stands," Manaen reminded us. "The city is contaminated. Jesus will not enter it."

I groaned and turned away.

Chuza searched Manaen's face until he seemed satisfied. Then he spoke. "This healer from Nazareth is no fool."

CHAPTER NINE

Then Mary said, "Here am I, the servant of the Lord."
—*Luke* 1:38

Pilate and his wife, Procula, stopped in Tiberias on a tour of the provinces. It was a brief visit, but I welcomed every distraction. In the days since Manaen returned from Capernaum with news of Jesus, I avoided Antipas. A visit from Pilate would occupy him a bit longer. I did not look forward to explaining my healer's refusal to obey Antipas's command and come to Tiberias. There was no excuse for such defiance, however many I invented.

Pilate's arrival at Antipas's court was a mixed blessing. Rivals, they would have declared their mutual loathing long ago, except that they lived by the same rule—there are no permanent enemies and no permanent friends among rulers. This visit was just another test of the limits.

I suppose Pilate knew about the vicious letter Antipas wrote to Caesar. I found out when Manaen confided to Chuza. It seems the tetrarch returned from his last stay in Jerusalem and found something new to criticize about Pilate's ability to rule. He wrote to complain that Jerusalem, Rome's crown jewel of the Eastern Empire, was in a shambles.

Whether I approved of Manaen's spies or not, I did gloat over the gossip they provided. Antipas's letter accused Pilate of failing to keep the public buildings as clean as they should be. It was just another attempt to win favor at Pilate's expense.

The morning of Pilate's arrival in Tiberias, his wife, Procula, was the brightest face in the governor's party. Her royal chin had expanded to a triple roll, forcing the garnet necklace she wore to tighten, noticeably. I was fascinated by her dress, an embroidered affair ending in a flounce. I suppose it was the latest in Cordoba.

The governor's gigantic head turned sluggishly on his stooped shoulders. He was a drowsy tortoise in Roman uniform. As my husband and I were announced, Antipas waved to Chuza, calling him closer. We crossed the courtyard and made our official greetings.

Herodias barely seemed to recognize us but stared blankly. Perhaps Procula sensed my lack of rapport with the tetrarch's wife. She took my arm, and from that moment I gave her my undivided attention.

"Joanna," she began, all suggestion and surprise.

"You will be so jealous," she squealed. "Nicolas has been to my house."

Everything excited Procula. "My dining room walls are now painted with the most exquisite vista of the Roman countryside," she burbled. "You've never seen so many grapes."

"How patriotic."

"Have you heard about Julia?"

The mention of Caesar's wife drew me in.

"She invited me to visit her in Rome," Procula sighed. "I've heard her villa is in the richest taste."

I could see my companion building up to something.

"But can you imagine," she said, "a woman like that, alone in Rome while her husband lives in Capri?"

Rumor was that Julia had contracted syphilis and Tiberius Caesar had nothing to do with it. His only interest in Rome seemed to be the constant supply of houseboys it had to offer. A fresh boatload set sail for Capri every month.

"She rarely goes to see him," Procula whispered. "It's a shame." I nodded in sympathy but said nothing.

"And you, dear child. How do you manage to look so well?"

Drawn to her flattery, I was about to answer when her eyes widened and she twirled her wrist in the air between us. "I remember," she said. "The healer you told me about—what was his name? He has cured you, hasn't he!"

"Very good, my lady," Antipas answered. He had crept up on us. "We have our own miracle cure right here at court," he said. "Tell us, Joanna, what has become of the healer?"

I tried to say something, anything, but no words came to me. Antipas turned on his heel, swept around and called Chuza. "My steward knows everything," he said in a shrill voice. "What can you tell us about your wife's healer, Chuza? I've been expecting him."

"I sent word," my husband answered, apparently untroubled. "Jesus the Nazarene says that he cannot enter Tiberias."

The tetrarch's smile began to crack and slide. My husband calmly finished the news. "It is a violation of Hebrew law."

"Violation?" Antipas's voice was the shattering sound of breaking glass. "Violation of what law?" The tetrarch turned to me. He knew that Hebrews avoided his capital city because he built it on an ancient cemetery. He seemed to want a better explanation.

"Who is this healer from Nazareth?" Antipas sneered. "How does he dare refuse his ruler?" Mumbling to himself, he let slip a deranged giggle. "You should have told me about this sooner, Chuza," he said, almost as if he were teasing my husband. "Now I'll have to wonder why my steward would keep such news from me."

In front of the entire assembled court, with Pilate as a witness, Antipas had actually dared to insinuate my husband's disloyalty. No one remarked on it. They stood by, worrying about their own fate. Antipas could turn on anyone, at any time.

"It's cold," Pilate grumbled, indifferently. "I'm going inside."

Before I left the palace that day, I passed Procula once again. She asked if I would accompany her to the mineral springs during her visit. She had heard about a private source for women, owned by two sisters, on a family estate they had inherited. The mention of the steaming muck was discouraging.

"I would be honored," I said with a bow.

"We haven't had enough time," she said. Her flirtatious eyes sparkled.

At home, Chuza and I spent our evening in the green room, warming ourselves against the chilling events of the day. I was completely undone by Antipas's behavior.

"Tell me again," I said, nestled on the couch beside my husband. "What, exactly, did you say to Antipas about Jesus?"

Chuza clamped his hands to his sides to discourage me from pressing closer to him. "You're being ridiculous," he said. "I told him the truth."

"But what do you know about religious burial laws?"

"Very little."

"You spoke as if you are an expert."

"I listen to my workers in Sepphoris, that is how I know," Chuza said. "Some of the best carpenters and builders refuse to work in Tiberias, no matter how much they need the money. They would rather starve."

Chuza was accustomed to Antipas's tests. I longed to paw at every detail. More than anything, I hoped for reassurance that Antipas would give up trying to lure Jesus to court. I leaned against my husband, reassured by his strength.

The next day as I approached the steaming mineral springs, I thought this must be how the mythical boatman, Charon, was supposed to feel when he ferried the condemned to the underworld. Vapors rose off the water as they surely must rise from the river of woe. I entered there like a woman banished to the place of death and terrible dreams.

My purpose held me steady. I had to impress upon Claudia Procula the truth about my healer. She could help him, perhaps even be an ally, if only she understood.

We met early in the day at the secluded pool. I knew the sisters who owned the estate. Their father had been Antipas's chief goldsmith until he reached very old age. They used their inheritance to treat women who suffered from every sort of ailment. They were convinced that their mineral bath was medicinal.

A warm mist hovered over the water. Procula removed her linen robe to expose skin the color of a pistachio shell. I went toward the pool, the short hairs around my forehead tightened in the steam.

Sliding out of my robe, I uncovered a body that would have shamed me during the long years of my illness. But now I revealed my plump shoulders and rounded curves as proof that I had been restored to health. Gliding into the water, tilting my chin to avoid the oily surface, I floated for a time and then returned to the steps to sit in the shallows. Small waves lapped over us, and Procula swished her hands in them.

For me it was not a pleasant pastime. I consider matters of health and grooming to be private. The world of sulfur springs and rejuvenating mud was foreign to me. But for Procula it was a religious experience.

I tried to imagine my cousin Mary wading into a hot springs. I felt all the more certain that I did not belong there.

We rose from our thick stew. Procula wrapped herself in a robe, blissful. We were bundled in our soft blankets, resting on our couches, and still the only sounds she made were contented coos.

Her eyes were closed when she spoke. "Now, then," she said, letting one listless arm fall over the edge of her couch. "Tell me."

I began, hurrying through the details of my healing, forging onward to the more important matter of my healer.

"Jesus," I began. My voice wavered with emotion. "He is not a proud man." I could never seem to find the words to describe him. "There are so many miracle workers in Galilee and Judea, but he is not like the others."

"I am sure he is not," Procula answered, encouraging me.

"Some people say he is the greatest prophet who ever lived."

Procula's eyes shot open.

"Did he predict your future?"

I was not making myself clear. "What I mean is, he doesn't only care about people who have power and titles," I said. "He helps the people everyone else despises. You can't blame him if he refused to enter Tiberias. It is just that he wants to avoid trouble."

"Blame him? I admire him," Procula said. "Who wouldn't like to avoid Herod Antipas?"

She had no idea of what I was trying to say. I quietly asked the God of mercy to let Claudia Procula remember the name of Jesus, and think well of him.

When we were leaving the springs, Procula surveyed the servants who waited for us in the shade. "Isn't that girl from the palace?" she asked, turning toward me so as not to be overheard.

I looked at the faces before us but did not recognize any of the tetrarch's household.

"Which one?" I asked, following her gaze.

"With the eyebrows," Procula said, drawing a double arch in front of us.

"That is my maidservant, Octavia."

Procula frowned, as if that could not be right. "I saw her last evening from my window," she said.

"My maidservant was with me," I assured her. I was not about to let anyone imply that I manage an undisciplined house. "We were packing for Sepphoris." I reviewed the evening from memory. Octavia and I worked together after dinner, and we both retired at the usual time.

"Well, then," Procula said, "perhaps I noticed her at the morning reception. Who could forget those eyebrows?"

"Of course," I said, to set her at ease. I was certain that she was mistaken.

Several days later, Chuza and I finally set out for Sepphoris. With so much strain and conflict during the long winter months, I was grateful for the chance to get away. In the year since my healing I had worn a mask, a false expression I hid behind whenever I was near Antipas. I pretended that I was no different than before, except that my health was restored.

I didn't want him to know that I had become a follower of
Jesus.

I had also tried to convince my husband that there was no
harm in my decision. I wanted to believe that it had no
bearing on Chuza's reputation at court. He knew otherwise,
and although he did not demand that I avoid my healer and
his friends, he warned me there would be a price to pay.

My disgruntled maidservant worried me, as well. I could not
think of any slave of Antipas's who resembled Octavia enough
for Procula to get confused. What, then, was Octavia doing at
the palace without me? My impatience with court life was
dulling my sharp wits. No one can afford to make that mistake.

These thoughts weighed on me as we passed the dusty olive
leaves that waved us on toward Sepphoris. We were home,
but home was not the escape I wished it could be.

I made plans to visit my cousin at her first free moment.
My husband and I had agreed that I would not return to Capernaum, but Nazareth was acceptable.

Our first few days at home, Chuza was not himself. He
went out to the fields despite poor digestion. I did not try to
convince him to stay in bed. I told myself he would soon
improve, now that he was far away from Antipas.

Several weeks later, when Chuza was with the field-workers,
Octavia and I rode to Nazareth. My relations with my maidservant remained uneasy. I resolved to talk through our dif-
fereces as we rode along, and to reach an agreement with her.

I raised the question of her freedom. "I know it is what you
want," I began.

She was completely confident that she had a right to expect her liberty.

"I've given it some thought," I continued. "And discussed it with your master." The troubling episodes of late winter in Tiberias made Octavia's request seem minor in comparison.

"At the time of my death you will have your freedom," I said. "I will leave you well enough provided for that you can support yourself from then on."

I thought my offer was more than fair. Octavia was five years younger than me. That gave her ample time to taste the delights of supporting herself, after I was gone.

She stared out the window, letting her fingers rub the nubby woven belt she wore as she watched the farmers pull weeds from a cotton field. After some consideration she answered without enthusiasm. "Thank you," she said. "You have always been generous."

The road outside Nazareth was unusually crowded. We climbed the switchback slowly, passing many people on foot. Closer to Mary's house, Phineas began whistling through his teeth to clear our path.

Simon, the bully, met us at the gate to my cousin's family compound and offered us a grudging welcome before he stepped aside to let us enter.

My cousin did not come to her door. I looked back at Simon. "Knock," he said.

Phineas did as we were told. The door opened, and my cousin stood back to let us inside. I asked the servants to wait and motioned to a shaded porch on the second level.

"Mary of Nazareth," someone called from the gate. Simon blocked the woman's entrance.

My cousin smiled and waved kindly but did not go out to meet the woman. She looked as if she did not have the strength for it.

The house was crowded with what appeared to be other people's belongings. It was so unlike my cousin to live with a disorderly mess.

"People bring gifts," she said. There was none of her usual lightness.

"What is all of it for?" I asked.

"They come here asking me to speak to my son about them." Her eyes cast around the room. "I see as many of them as I can."

I pulled back the curtain to her storage cave and peered into a place filled with chipped wooden bowls, thinning lengths of rope, a small cart with wheels more square than round. The gifts, I concluded.

I made us strong ginger tea to revive us. We sat together on a corner bench. My cousin's face was all sharp peaks and sunken valleys. She spoke with some effort.

"I don't sleep," she said.

Simon pushed open the door. "The old widower is here," he said. "What do I tell him?"

My cousin pressed the back of her hand against her cheek to hold in place what vitality she had left.

"I will see him at the well."

"He'll want to know how long," Simon answered.

"Not long."

"Why don't I send him away?"

Mary insisted that she would meet the man, later on.

The tea made some difference; my cousin stood and walked to her kitchen, pointing to the water jugs. I picked one up, she took it from me and sent me back for another. As soon as we were outside, I called Phineas.

"Follow closely behind us," I said quietly. "Don't let anyone interrupt us."

We walked the narrow streets. Townspeople watched us, but the massive shadow that Phineas cast held them at a distance.

"People come here from across the whole world," Mary said. "Persia, Egypt. Some think my son is Elijah, one of the greatest of the prophets, reborn."

"What do you tell them?"

"I say no, but they have made up their mind."

We rounded the last turn on the road to the well. An older man hurried toward my cousin as if he had been waiting. He reached for her bucket, leaned over the rim and dropped the bucket into the depths. Then he cranked it back to the surface and smiled at her.

"It went as you said," he began awkwardly. "I went to the widow's house, and she has agreed."

My cousin nodded and smiled her approval.

The old man watched me as he spoke. "My brother's widow," he said. "She has agreed to marry me. The prophet's mother spoke to her about me."

He insisted on carrying the water jugs back to Mary's house but walked behind us with Phineas.

Simon was repairing a plough at the door of his shop. "It's always like this now," he said, not looking up from his work. "People bring their troubles here, every little request. We have enough problems of our own."

All that day, Simon turned away callers at the gate. Some left a modest gift along with their request. It was only his belligerence that kept them from walking into the house.

To amuse my cousin I described my trip to the hot springs with Procula, the governor's wife. It was a dank place that promised health and rejuvenation, but I did not feel anything, I told her.

Mary went to the door and motioned for me to follow. We went back in the direction of the well but stopped at a small hut set back from the road. She opened a low gate and led me into a clean place with narrow benches against the walls. Clear water flowed into a small, steep pool. I had seen huts like it all of my life, but never been inside.

There was no sound except spring water trickling into the pool.

"This is our way to become clean in the sight of the Lord," she said. "When we wash in this water, we are prepared to begin again. We have made things right between us and our Maker. Your ancestors did the same, until some of them left the holy ways behind. Now it is for you to decide, whether to return to their customs or not."

I took off my robe and descended into the water, lingered

in the water's embrace and then surfaced. Mary put her arms out to help me. I dressed quickly. We sat on the bench. For my cousin, this water was sacred. For Procula, a mineral pool had its powers. Was one choice right and the other wrong? I could not be the judge. Having been raised with no religion, I could only be grateful that I had found my way, at last.

CHAPTER TEN

...Chuza, the manager of Herod's household.

—Luke 8:3

L ate in spring, my world began to resemble endless dusk. Chuza was the source of this dull light. His health wavered. And while he denied it, his skin had turned the gray color of a man with a wasting disease. He had lapses where he could not warm himself, no matter how close he sat to the fire.

One morning I was counting silver plates and goblets with the housekeeper in our monthly inventory when Chuza entered the dining room, upset that he could not find his ledger. I reminded him that he was carrying it on his way to bed last night. He insisted it was not in its usual place. My husband's record book contained every detail of planting and weather that he relied on from year to year. We searched the house. When I found the missing book, on the floor under his couch, he scowled as if I were to blame. Neither of us said any more about it.

Each evening Chuza had less appetite. He refused to eat anything but watery stews. I finally sent for his Roman doctors, who put him on a diet of bland white fish to settle his stomach and a daily herb drink with mint to sharpen his memory. By midsummer he said he was improving, but his liquid eyes and ashen face told me otherwise.

Days spent out of doors with the field-workers gave Chuza's cheeks and his arms the polished look of health. But we were soon confronted with his ailing.

I was with Strabo, overseeing the harvest of my first crop of strawberries. I had managed to coax just a few from the ground after Joseph brought me several plants from Gaul, at great expense. We were getting to be old friends, he and I. As he opened his trove of spices on visits to my house, he always managed a few questions about my cousin Mary. The truth was, she saw far more of him than I did, from what I could tell. I never let on to him that I knew it.

Preoccupied with my miserable berry crop, I did not hear Phineas enter the storage house.

"The master is coming in from the fields," he said with some urgency.

"Is anything wrong?" I untied my apron and wiped the grit from around my fingernails.

"Two of his men are carrying him." We went quickly to the

front gate. There were three men coming toward the house. Chuza was slumped between the others.

My husband's men brought him inside. One of them told me that Chuza had been passing blood. The back of his tunic was stained.

They placed him on his bed as if he were as fragile as glass. When I covered him with a linen blanket, his face tightened in pain. Even that small weight was too much for him.

For many uncertain days I fed my husband a few bites of sweetened curd as often as he would allow it. He could not always keep the food down, even though he ate very little.

Several evenings, when I went to the kitchen to get him a draught to help him sleep, long after old Bernice had retired for the evening, I met Octavia there. She needed oil for her lamp or she wanted to be sure the windows were closed. Each time she asked after Chuza, but I was too distracted to offer more than a word or two.

It was odd, finding her in the kitchen so often. I supposed she planned it, as her way of telling me that she was ready to help.

One evening at my husband's bedside I held the cup for him to sip, but he stopped my hand and spoke, with terrible effort.

"Tomorrow I am going to send word to Manaen," he said. "The men can't go unsupervised."

"Of course."

"He will take care of things until I am able."

"Promise me that you will stop worrying when he comes."

Chuza relaxed into his pillows.

It seemed unfair to question his plan, convinced though I was that Manaen would take advantage of my husband's condition.

"There is no one else I can trust," Chuza said. "The grapes are ready to be harvested."

I sat beside my husband, planning arrangements for our guest. Manaen would have a proper welcome, but I would trust him no more than a gull trusts the fish she hovers over, ready to pluck it from the water.

My husband's friend arrived surrounded by his guards and valets. I had seen his display often enough, but once again I was taken in by the show of iron and animal hides.

When he bowed, just so, I blushed, and hated myself for it.

"The Royal Steward looks forward to seeing you," I said, making a point of using my husband's title, to remind Manaen of his place.

I was about to lead him to Chuza's rooms, but he stood looking down at the ground, waiting for something more.

"He is eager to speak to you," I said.

Glancing around to be sure his men were not close, Manaen took a small black stone from his pocket and held it out to me. I couldn't imagine what it was for. It reminded me of the black stone buildings of Capernaum.

"It is from the courtyard of the teacher's house," Manaen said. "I took it with me."

It was not clever of him to remind me of his recent, failed journey north. He had lingered there far too long and returned without Jesus, which was the whole purpose for the trip. I am certain Antipas took it as a personal insult and blamed Chuza.

I smiled my official smile and slowly looked upon the rock in my hand.

"Thank you," I said.

"It was a very important trip for me," he said.

"Isn't it unfortunate, the way it turned out." I knew it was harsh of me, but I was still angry at him for failing us.

I walked with him to Chuza's rooms and continued down the hall to my own quarters, where I busied myself by sorting through old dresses and cloaks. I had fallen into the habit of sending Phineas to Capernaum whenever circumstances allowed him to deliver my castoffs to the house where my healer stayed.

Manaen did not leave Chuza's side for some time. I grew restless and went across the courtyard to check once again on his quarters. Not that I was searching for anything in particular. I only wanted to see that he had nothing of a suspicious nature in his luggage. On the floor beside his satchel there was a roll of pages tied with a leather cord. Since it was not hidden, I felt it must not be a secret. I only wanted to be sure.

The first two or three sheets contained drawings of the fields around Sepphoris. Entire plots of land were marked off with the history of the crops planted in them, and a note about which grain, which vegetable, was planted where during the past seven years. Cabbage, onion, beans. My husband must have asked for the records—they were the kind of thing he would study and discuss for hours.

I flipped from page to page and was about to roll up the stack when a smaller drawing slipped out. It was a beautiful work, an artist's rendering of a box made of stone. Two sides were decorated with symbols. Unmistakable images, I slowly began to see. There was a royal crest with a scales and abacus, a walking stick made of an olive branch and a stately chair with arms that resemble those of a powerfully made man.

Each symbol represented my husband. These were Chuza's courtly emblems, the implements of his office. My fingers played nervously with the edges of the page. It was a drawing of an ossuary, one that must have been intended for my husband's bones after he died.

Footsteps outside the room brought me back to my surroundings. I tied the leather string around the roll, placed it where I had found it and rushed to the window as if I were adjusting the shutters against the light.

Manaen opened the door and I turned.

"Forgive me for entering," I said, quite breathless. "I wanted to be sure your rooms were in order."

He looked carefully at his belongings before he spoke. "They seem to be."

"How did you find the Royal Steward?"

"How long has he been like this?"

"Like this?"

It was improper of Manaen to close the door to his room before continuing our conversation, but I allowed it, not wanting to risk the servants overhearing us.

"He is extremely ill."

"He insists he is improving and will soon be himself."

"I've seen others in his condition."

"What condition do you mean?"

He was watching me intently. I had the feeling he was about to accuse me of something.

"Your husband is being poisoned," he said.

The chair beside me was in reach, but I did not get to it before I fell. The next thing I remember, Manaen was lifting me off the floor. His face was so close that I could see a deep frown between his eyes, and his twisted mouth.

"It's all right," I said, pulling myself upright in the chair.

He stood over me, waiting I am sure for me to tell him how it was that Chuza became so ill.

"The Royal Steward told me that he has been losing strength for some time," Manaen said, cold as a lawyer.

He glared as if he were preparing to restrain me in any way he found necessary. He had turned into a ready weapon before my eyes. I half expected him to call his guards and have me dragged away. On what charges I feared to think.

"I am putting this household under my supervision," he announced. The words flew at me. "I will start by interrogating your kitchen staff, and then anyone who has had access to the Royal Steward's rooms. Where is your head cook?"

"Bernice?"

He did not so much as pause out of courtesy, let alone goodwill, before he advised me of my own situation. "No one is to leave this house without my permission," he said. "Not you or anyone else."

"Are you accusing me of trying to harm my husband?" I shouted.

I was incensed.

"I don't know who is or is not responsible," he said. "But I will find out."

I rushed to Chuza, terrified that Manaen might have upset him. Outside my husband's room I stopped long enough to quiet my loud breathing. Distressing situations still brought on a hint of the old rattle.

"Joanna?" he called. It was grim music, the sound of Chuza's voice. But at least he was still alive.

I leaned close to his tepid cheek as he spoke in a whisper.

"I want to see my brother," he said. "Send for Cyrus."

I only wished we had sent for him sooner. I called Phineas and met him in Chuza's library, the room where he did his official work. My servant's eyes soon fixed on my hair. I put my hand to it and understood. The whole arrangement had fallen loose.

"I must take you into my confidence," I began. I was about to say that he had been a good and trustworthy servant, but the memory of Manaen's harsh warning gave me pause. He was right, of course. All of us were suspects. "Please, Phineas," I said. "Don't let us down."

My servant nodded in obedience and waited for my instructions.

"Go to Cyrus, my husband's brother. Tell him that the steward is near death. Tell him the cause appears to be..." I could not bring myself to say it. "Tell him he must bring his medicine box."

I could only hope that my brother-in-law was spending his summer in Tyre as usual, to give his annual lectures. Phineas promised that he could get there and back in five days. My sudden tears were my only answer. He took my hand and pressed it to his forehead.

"May the Almighty One protect you," I said.

Manaen stepped into the room. He had been listening. I should have expected it.

"What are you doing?" he asked. It so unnerved me that I offered every detail of my plan.

"You should have come to me," he said. "Tell me where to find the doctor. I'll send one of my men."

Phineas stood waiting for some further instruction. I was humiliated and could barely face him. "Thank you, Phineas," I said. "You won't be needed."

I was growing accustomed to Manaen's glare and managed to allow him to watch me, as if I were an insect pinched on prongs.

"I have removed your kitchen staff," he announced. "My own staff will be here by tomorrow morning to replace them."

"Not Bernice," I groaned in disbelief. "She couldn't harm anyone."

"She is confined to her room like everyone else," he said without a hint of sympathy.

I could not blame Manaen. I had considered doing the same when I first noticed my husband's failing health. I sensed an enemy in my house, sensed it and denied the possibility all at once.

Manaen held my entire kitchen staff for questioning. He also placed Chuza's Roman doctors under house arrest until he could question them. He took their medicine boxes from them and put them aside, until he could bring in a doctor he knew and trusted to review them. An empty granary became the household prison.

The day after he arrived, he entered my rooms as if he had every right.

"Who is Phineas?" he demanded.

"He has been with us since we were first married," I said. "He came to us from my mother's staff."

Manaen took a note on his tablet. "I'll see him alone now," he said. He asked about Chuza's valets, and he told me he had interrogated Strabo and placed him in prison.

"For what?" I all but shrieked.

"Until I can check every inch of these grounds to be certain that no poisonous root or herb or berry is being cultivated here, your gardeners will be confined," Manaen answered.

I held my head, not sure what to do. An earthquake was ripping my household apart. And I was powerless to stop it.

He went away, but not for long.

Just after dinner, Manaen came to my pantry. I was sorting though the shelves to see what food I might need from storage. Six of his staff followed me everywhere, as if I were a thief.

"Your maidservant," Manaen demanded. "Who is she?"

His battering manner and the serious nature of his questions burst a floodgate inside me. I told him everything I could think of about Octavia: how I had found her in the kitchen so often, how she had asked for her freedom and remained in a sullen mood ever since I refused her, how I had heard rumors that she went alone to Antipas's villa without my knowing.

Manaen was on his feet. "Take me to her," he said.

"She said she would be in the laundry room, mending some of my things."

He started out the door, motioning me to lead the way.

I felt a chill come over me. The skin on my arms rose up in tiny bumps. We went to the laundry room. There was no one there but Bernice. She'd been released from confinement and found a way to make herself useful.

We went through the kitchen, stripped of all familiarity. Guards covered each entrance. I led the way to my rooms, where Octavia and I had been working earlier in the day. I called her name as I entered. No answer. In Chuza's rooms my husband dozed. But Manaen held his fingers beneath Chuza's nose to satisfy himself that my husband was alive.

We left him and went on to Octavia's room. Manaen knocked, then he pushed the door open. None of her belongings were in their place. No cloak or tunic hung on the peg. Her comb and the shells she carried with her since childhood were not on the shelf. The small carving of Hera was gone from its niche.

Manaen ordered that every building on the property be searched. One of his kitchen staff said that Octavia went out toward the orchard just after dinner. She was carrying a large basket.

"Why didn't you tell me?" he shot back at the servant. The man looked at him dumbly. He hadn't thought of it, obviously.

Manaen turned to one of his guards, never more than a step or two behind him.

"Take this man to the prison," he said.

It was brutal. There was no talking to him.

For Chuza's sake, I would have prepared a basket from my kitchen and sent it to Capernaum, with a message asking my healer to come and help us. But I could not do so without my husband's permission, and I had not found a way to ask him.

For my sake, therefore, I prepared a basket with almond oil, ripe figs and a pouch filled with dried dill. I prepared a message to accompany it, asking Mary to come as quickly as possible.

I went to Manaen's quarters with my request. I was not prepared for what I found there. He had turned his quarters into a command post. His table faced the door and was crowded with tablets and diagrams of the fields. Other diagrams were pinned to the wall like strategy maps.

Passing the guard, I entered.

"May I send this basket to my cousin and ask that she come to me?" I began, trying to keep my voice steady despite my terror.

Manaen hardly bothered to look up. "No outsiders," he said.

I spoke again, less confidently.

"You know my cousin," I said. "Mary, the mother of Jesus."

His expression changed. I believe I saw a look of true affection. He motioned me to hand him the basket, lifted the linen and inspected the contents.

"Leave it here," he said. "One of my men will take it to her."

"You will need directions," I replied, pleased to point out his oversight.

"I know the house."

Whatever brought him to Nazareth, I did not presume to ask. I had no such privileges. I was a prisoner in my own home.

"Then I will leave it to you," I said.

From the time those words dropped reluctantly from my lips I was in constant prayer, if begging and pleading counts as prayer. I went to my rooms each day and closed the door to spend time alone. Determined as I was to call upon the Holy One, I did not know where to begin.

At first I watched the clouds outside my window and the workers climbing the apricot trees in our orchard. The branches bent low where the little boys stood to reach for the ripe fruit.

I recited a few lines of a prayer I had committed to memory, holding Chuza in my heart as I prayed.

Hear, O Lord, and answer me

for I am poor and needy.

Guard my life

I am devoted to you.

Save the servant who loves you.

* * *

On one such day, rather than begin with my usual flood of complaints, I sat quietly. I heard the buzz of the locusts and the distant voices of the field-workers. The clatter of the servants moving through the house gradually faded. A sense of rest, I could call it peace, came over me. More than that, I felt that I was not alone. The Creator of all life was with me. I could almost hear that sacred breath.

Such harmony did not last, but it was enough to draw me back to my rooms each day. I grew more certain that the Holy One was with us and would not leave us to our own defenses. I had learned one hard lesson about a life of faith. I have no control over what will be. All I can do is choose to trust, or not.

One afternoon I went from my prayers to my husband's bedside. I sat near him, and after some time he opened his eyes, squinting painfully at the late afternoon light.

"Do you remember when Jesus came here?" I asked.

Chuza looked down at the rumpled sheet covering his chest. There were tiny drops of blood on it, from his most recent convulsion.

"We saw how he heals the sick. I have never been seriously ill since that night."

My husband looked at me to show me that he was paying attention. But he did not answer.

"I want to ask him to come back—for you. I know he will help us."

Chuza shook his head, just slightly. It was all he could manage, but it was enough to tell me he was against the idea.

"He will not ask you to be his follower. He helped me when I hardly knew him."

My husband touched one finger to his lips to quiet me. I sat beside him, wondering what to say that might have some influence.

We sat together for a time. Chuza spoke once more.

"You say He is the God of mercy. Then we will leave it for Him to decide where I spend my eternity."

Each time Manaen went to my husband's room, I found myself hovering near the door. Cyrus was due to arrive. I was disappointed each time I went to the roof looking for a sign of him. In those days, too, I learned that my cousin was in Capernaum and would not soon return to Nazareth.

In the kitchen I prepared my husband's meager food. Rather, I should say, I described the steps. Manaen's cook did the work. If I went toward the storage to get honey or reached to stir the pot, I was ordered away.

I tolerated such vile treatment for as long as I could and then went to make my complaint. An armed guard, an escort I had grown accustomed to, brought me to the roof. Manaen was watching the road. He motioned his men to leave us alone and took one last look to the north before he turned toward me.

"The doctor should have been here by now," he said. I thought I heard a suggestion of human emotion.

"I found something," I said. "I want to ask you about it."

He looked mildly curious.

"A drawing."

He broadened his shoulders, just slightly, like a man preparing for physical combat.

"In your room, the day you arrived. It was on the floor."

He showed no sign of understanding and let me go on stumbling through my speech.

"I believe it is a sketch for a burial box."

He didn't answer.

"Surely you noticed. It is covered with my husband's official emblems."

He chose his words carefully. "I've seen it."

"Where did it come from?"

A sudden loud whistle interrupted us. Manaen turned toward the road. In the distance, just before the way curves inward between the hills, two large torches waved through the air.

"They are here," Manaen called over the wall to the guards below us. "Ride out to meet them. Signal me as soon as you reach them."

He went briskly past me toward the stairs, startled to find me still there.

"The drawing," he said. "I will tell you soon what I can." He ordered the guards to stay with me as he passed them.

My brother-in-law was noticeably worn from his travels. The cart he rode in, however, held promise. It was tightly packed with every healing salve and poultice known to his profession.

I met him and his escort as they entered the gate. Cyrus smelled of pine-scented water, which he always applied liberally when attempting to refresh himself. The scent was as much a part of him as his fringe of dark hair and his clean fingernails. But it was not strong enough to cover the grime he carried in from the road. I was deeply touched by his efforts. He had traveled hard for Chuza's sake.

I embraced my brother-in-law, never happier to see him. He lifted his medicine box and told his guards to put his cart in a shaded place, and not to touch anything until he was present. We hurried into the house. I asked a servant to bring a fresh jug of water to my husband's rooms.

Chuza opened his eyes at the sound of Cyrus's steps. He tried to sit up, but Cyrus went to him, sparing him the strain, and gently raised my husband's feverish head to ruffle the back of his hair and cool him.

He set to work, pressing carefully on Chuza's chest, lifting his eyelids to expose his watery eyes, observing his blue-tipped fingernails as the first steps in examining him.

"When did it begin?" Cyrus asked.

"Soon after we arrived home from Tiberias," Chuza whispered.

"Why did you wait so long?"

"I thought it would go away."

Seeing the two of them together, I recognized the truth.

Chuza, once a heartier version of his ascetic brother, had been reduced to a shadow of Cyrus.

Several days later I called for Phineas. He had been cleared of suspicion and was free to do whatever I asked.

"In the morning, after you have eaten, go to the house of my cousin, the mother of my healer," I said.

He almost smiled. Phineas rarely smiled at anything.

"Ask whoever you find there when she is expected to return. Offer to escort her to Sepphoris as soon as she is able to travel. Tell them that the Royal Steward is gravely ill."

I went to my garden and watched the shadows creep irreversibly across the wall. My husband's brother was with him. Manaen was bringing in the grape harvest, and he would not rest until he found Octavia. I had done all that I could. I needed my cousin to keep me strong.

The next day, as usual, I supervised meals for Cyrus and Manaen, making sure that the kitchen ran to my satisfaction, and I waited for word from Nazareth. Before the evening meal, Phineas returned.

We went to the garden where the enclosing walls gave me the feeling, real or imagined, that I was protected.

"Your cousin has been delayed in Capernaum," Phineas began. He was so unaccustomed to long speeches, he stepped back as if that was all he intended to say.

"But whom did you meet in Nazareth?" I asked.

"I spoke first to Joses."

Joses, the gentle one, was nothing like his brother Simon.

"What did he say?"

"Your cousin is expected in two days."

"Did you hear anything else in Nazareth?"

"Yes," Phineas said. Then he fell silent again and waited to be asked.

"What did you hear? Please, tell me everything."

"They were talking at the well," he said. "Your cousin's son, the teacher, had been to see his mother. Some neighbors tried to throw him off the cliff."

In the painstaking interview that followed, my servant explained, drop by drop, that Jesus had restored the sight of a blind man from the town. When he said it was the power of the Almighty in him, the neighbors were outraged.

I tried to imagine Mary, hurrying to be with her son, knowing he was in some other danger in Capernaum, I supposed. I thanked my servant. From then on I told myself that I must not expect my cousin to come to Sepphoris. Loneliness grew within me. A terrible sadness filled my days.

My brother-in-law and I crossed paths in Chuza's rooms or in the hallway, but Cyrus offered no report about my husband except to say that nothing had changed. Finally, one evening he sent word that he wished to see me. I arranged to meet him in the small room off the entrance to the house and went to wait for him there.

I opened the window to allow in the scent of the garden. Cyrus arrived promptly and brought with him the added aroma of pine trees.

The lines across his forehead deepened as he spoke.

"For some time now," he said, "my brother has been fed small doses of arsenic."

My hand rose up to cradle my cheek. I craved human touch, even my own, to steady me.

"Will he recover?" I asked.

Cyrus did not waste one breath trying to console me.

"Most likely, no," he said. "His body fluids are amber—they should be pale yellow."

"What will we do?" I asked.

"I've given him crushed citrus seed, and I have tried bezoar solutions to draw out the poison. It has worked in some cases, but I am not encouraged by the results here. You have seen with what difficulty he breathes. And the convulsions are more frequent in the last several days. Each one cuts off more of his strength."

"Has Manaen told you how this happened?" I asked. Cyrus must know about Octavia. Otherwise he would be treating me like a suspect.

"Yes, your maidservant."

"My maidservant," I repeated, hoping to reduce my shame by saying it out loud.

"I am sorry."

I could see that he was struggling for something more to say. Finally he managed, "You have been a good wife to my brother."

I left Cyrus and went to Manaen's rooms. I had heard him crossing the courtyard while I was with my brother-in-law.

He opened the door and allowed me to enter.

"My husband is dying," I said. "You lied to me."

He leaned back on his desk and watched me, as if I were a small but feisty animal, a ferret trapped but hoping to scare him with my squeaky growl.

"I am the one who told you he was being poisoned."

"You knew it even before you came here."

He stood up. The pathetic little creature before him had managed to nick his heel.

"I didn't know," he said.

"You brought your own drawing of my husband's ossuary."

"I found that under my door, the morning I left Tiberias," he said, suddenly trying to defend himself.

"Where did it come from?"

He opened the wooden box on his desk and took out a small scroll. He held it without offering to show it to me.

"The drawing was inside this," he said. "There was a note, with the tetrarch's seal."

He unrolled the scroll and read. "'I will need a new steward by autumn. I am considering you.'"

"I don't believe you," I said.

He turned the scroll toward me. I recognized the large, uneven letters that slid downward, rather than straight across. It was the handwriting of Antipas.

"I brought it to show your husband," Manaen said.

"And, did you show him?"

"Yes."

Chuza knew, then, that he had been poisoned. Manaen had told him. That was why he sent for Cyrus.

"Help me," I moaned.

"We will find the one who did this," Manaen answered. The loyal captain of the guard, it was the best he could do to console me.

CHAPTER ELEVEN

Mary stayed with her.

—*Luke* 1:50

I expected my cousin every day, from the time Chuza's eyes rolled open in their final blindness. But even as I prepared to face his memorial ceremonies at Tiberias, Mary still had not left Capernaum.

My husband's funeral was a freakish display with crowds, eulogies and the deranged antics of Herod Antipas. A howling wind tormented the city, sending dead branches hurtling from the date palms like the feathers of monstrous birds.

Trumpets and the sudden outbursts of the processing horses reached my ears in muffled sounds. Shrouded, like my husband's entombed body.

Claudia Procula sent a letter of sympathy, and a rosebush

for my garden in Sepphoris. I was grateful that she did not come north for the occasion. I was in no condition to attend to her.

It was my cousin Mary I needed. Without her, I felt desperately alone.

Trying to ignore the circus atmosphere at the amphitheater, I looked out to the sapphire water and dreamed of distant places. Antipas's voice reeled me back.

"I loved him like a brother," he said, beating his breast.

"You murdered him," I said, hardly lowering my voice.

"A loyal servant of the Empire," Antipas wailed.

"Betrayed by the one he served," I corrected him.

He thrust his chest forward like a peacock. I closed my eyes and imagined myself making my way through the crowds to the stage, plunging a knife into him before a thousand witnesses.

The hours of speeches, the races and games, the tossing out of coins to the crowds...I survived them. Late in the day, the tetrarch came to me in one last flaunted betrayal. He stumbled forward, frothing at the mouth.

"I am sorry," he screeched. "I will miss him."

I watched my own teardrops stain my robe, not daring to meet his feverish stare.

When I returned to Sepphoris, I vowed never to set foot in Tiberias again.

We buried Chuza in my family's plot. Before the door of his tomb was sealed, I pressed my fingers against the inscription, my parting words to him. "We will meet again."

I spent most of that month in seclusion, wishing only to disappear from public life. Toward the end of it I received word that my cousin Mary was on her way to see me. Phineas went to escort her. I spent most of that day in my garden, face turned away from Tiberias. At midafternoon I went to the roof and watched the road.

I saw Mary first, riding a donkey with Phineas beside her. The travel bag she carried was smaller than what I usually take for a morning at the market. Yet, I knew that my cousin would remain with me for some time. When I was almost within reach of her, she slipped from the back of her beast and held out her arms to me. Her hair smelled of olive soap and the dusty underbrush of her travels.

"I came as soon as I could," she said.

"My husband," I began, not certain what more to say.

"Yes, I know."

She looked pale and lacked her usual vigor. I wondered if she had been ill, and therefore could not travel until now.

She nudged me forward, her arm around my waist, so that I would walk with her the short distance to the house. She did not try to explain her long absence, and it was not my place to ask her.

I chose the room across the hall from mine to be her room. The light is particularly pleasant there in morning. And I wanted her close enough to me so that I could hear her breathing through the night. Not long after she arrived, the sun disappeared behind the hills and the damp coolness of autumn settled into the house. I lit the furnace and before bed I warmed my cousin's blankets.

We went early to our separate rooms. She seemed weighted down by some trouble. I had begun to think about my cousin in a new way since my widowhood. The time would come when she, too, would no longer be with me. My solution to this sad awakening came without effort. I decided, quite intentionally, to take care of her for the rest of her life.

The next morning we rose before the sun, as she requested, and walked to my husband's tomb. My cousin seemed stronger than when she first arrived in Sepphoris. I attempted a conversation as we went along.

"You were in Capernaum," I said.

"Yes," she answered after some time.

"And you saw my healer."

"I stayed longer than I planned."

My cousin began to describe what sounded like a worrisome visit. She told several stories about her son and the temple authorities. One Sabbath Jesus went to dine with a prominent lawyer. On the way he healed a man who suffered fainting spells. Three of the temple elders questioned him about it.

"They asked him to name the most important of the laws," Mary said. "He recited them. They accused him of breaking the laws he knew so well."

She had to tell me, as I was not sure, that the most rigid observers believe it is better to let a suffering man die than to cure him on that day.

A fight broke out in the street, some defending my healer, others the religious authorities.

Mary stayed in Capernaum with her son for several weeks. During that time he told her he would go to Jerusalem for the Passover, less than two months away. Every enemy he ever made would be in the Holy City during the festival.

Her voice wavered. "He must think I have forgotten what he told me before he left home for the first time," she said. "He said he would not go to Jerusalem for the Passover again until he was ready to die."

"Surely he has changed his mind," I insisted. "He meant to say that he would return at last to the Holy City when he was old and ready to die." She did not answer me.

Several times during her stay in Sepphoris my cousin accompanied me to Chuza's tomb. At those times she stood beside me and said a prayer from memory.

I will give thanks to the Lord
With my whole heart,
In the company of the upright.
The works of his hands are
Faithful and just;
All his precepts are trustworthy.

Prayers for the dead are lacking. They fail to express the misery of those left behind. I filled in each line with my private complaints, asking the Almighty what sort of justice had been done to my husband.

Quite unexpectedly, an answer came to me. It seemed to have been there all along. The words were confident and wise.

"Look to the whole story, not the small part that each person plays."

A powerful charge gushed through me, as if some burst from on high had overtaken me. Once it passed, I toppled to the ground. My face pressed in the dirt, I listened to my cousin finish her prayer.

To revere the Lord is the beginning of wisdom.

Those who practice it have a good understanding.

His praise endures forever.

She helped me to my feet, steadied me, but did not ask what happened. I would have told her everything but sensed that she wished for me to learn that it is better to hold some mysteries in silence.

About one month into Mary's time with me, a stranger knocked at the door. It was a young man who wanted to invite my cousin to his wedding in Nazareth. I could see by the way he thanked her, again and again, that she had played her subtle part in arranging the engagement.

Several days later, a new mother arrived to show off her baby. Then a toothless old woman appeared, smiling broadly and offering two ears of corn. Before the end of the month, my cousin had visitors nearly every day. The numbers only increased after that.

There were gifts with each visit. Skeins of thread, a leaf

collection——I put them in Octavia's old room. It was good to find a useful purpose for that forsaken place.

When a family of five arrived at the house to see my cousin, they presented Mary with an empty jar, having used up the oil that it once contained. I recognized it, a jar from my own kitchen. After that I began to give one visitor's gift to the next, to make room for more.

Some who came were in visible states of distress. It was after sunset one evening when a barefoot woman with an evil eye tattooed on the palm of her hand banged on the door and disturbed the whole house. I came down to find two of my servants holding her by the arms, to prevent her from tearing through the room.

My cousin soon followed me and led the young woman into the small room near the entrance to the house. She brought a trail of dirty footprints with her, but no matter. I heard sobs of wretchedness, low murmurs, a deluge of tears, and then the door opened. The barefoot woman came out. My cousin looked at her as if to say it was all right. She walked the woman outside and returned without delay.

"She is looking for my son," Mary said.

"How did she find you?"

"She went to Nazareth. She has been to see me before."

Strangers came from as far as Ramah, asking for my cousin. We turned the front room into her reception area. I stationed servants near the door to keep watch. For the sake of her health I finally insisted that she see no more than two each day.

* * *

During the third month of my cousin's stay, Manaen arrived unexpectedly. I had not seen him since my husband's funeral and was surprised by how happy I was to meet him again. He had proved his loyalty to Chuza. He was welcome.

"I hope that you are improving," he said. A simple greeting, it was more convincing than his usual. The ordeal of my husband's illness had put an end to my bickering with Manaen. We had come to respect each other. I only recognized this as he stood before me, waiting to be invited in.

I led him to the garden, certain there was a reason for his visit, but he seemed in no hurry to explain himself and talked of his work and travels. When at last we were out of things to say, he sat forward in his chair.

"I have received word about your maidservant, Octavia," he said.

"Where is she?" I asked.

Manaen's answer was long and increasingly disturbing.

When she left Sepphoris, Octavia went quickly to Antipas's palace and stayed for some days, until passage to Athens was arranged for her. Antipas had promised her freedom as well as safe travel to her homeland and five gold pieces. In return, she murdered my husband.

"She sailed in early autumn," Manaen said. "I heard about her plans and sent a man to follow her. He returned to Tiberias a few days ago. I came directly to tell you."

I sat motionless in my chair, trying to understand. "What will become of her?" I asked.

"Octavia was murdered," Manaen said. "Strangled by a copper cord. It sliced through her neck and severed—"

I held up my hand up to hold back the awful details.

"She had no money among her possessions," Manaen said. "It was made to look as if it had been a robbery, but my man saw most of it. The assassin works for Antipas."

Manaen stayed with us for several days. He was as kind to my cousin as if she were his favorite aunt. I wondered how he knew her so well. As she and I were preparing supper one evening, I asked her.

"Has he been to see you in Nazareth?" I was grinding peppercorns for a stew.

"Not in some time." She did not so much as pause from her work, blending oil and flour with her fingers. "I last saw him in Capernaum this past winter."

"The teacher refused to meet Antipas," I said, reminded of that ill-fated trip.

"We were happy to see Manaen," she said.

I muttered something, not even aware that I was making noises.

"Did he tell you?" my cousin asked.

I shook my head no.

She stopped and considered me.

"He said he would tell you," she said.

In Capernaum, Manaen spoke privately to the teacher, and then he told everyone present that he was a disciple.

I listened to this account, half-distracted. I could not

remember where I had put that little black stone Manaen gave me on one of his visits to Sepphoris. He presented it, now that I recalled, just after his stay in Capernaum.

I went to the kitchen windowsill, the place where I stored such curiosities until I decided what to do with them. The stone was there, along with the key from a broken lamp.

We went to Manaen's rooms. I was ashamed of the way I had treated him so often in the past, and looked to my cousin to smooth things out.

"I told Joanna about your time in Capernaum," she began.

I held out the black stone, trying to say that I understood.

"I didn't know whether to tell you," he said. In the awkward smiles that followed I saw how the awful circumstances of Manaen's last stay in Sepphoris had forged a true friendship between us.

The night before Manaen left Sepphoris, he mentioned that he had seen the Master in Capernaum eight days earlier. He repeated something that he seemed to believe my cousin already knew.

"The teacher has left for Jerusalem," he said. "He will stop in the towns along the way and arrive in time for the Passover."

"When did this happen?" Mary asked. I could see that she did not know of her son's departure.

"I assumed he told you," Manaen said, half apologizing.

"I'll leave for Nazareth in the morning," Mary said. "I have to be in Jerusalem when my son is there."

Her determination may have seemed strange to Manaen. For my part, I understood at last the burden she carried in silence. Her son was going to meet his destiny. She wanted to be with him.

I did not say anything about my own intentions. The next morning I simply went to my room, took the small bag I had prepared and carried it to the front door. My cousin came down soon after. We left Sepphoris together.

CHAPTER TWELVE

When the days drew near for him to be taken up, he set his face to go to Jerusalem.

—*Luke* 9:51

Our caravan was made up of my cousin's relatives and neighbors. We rode south toward Jerusalem, planning to camp in nearby Bethphage during the festival. We added numbers to our group at each town. Many who joined us were related to those already among us. People rushed to one another's arms as if they had been counting the days until they could be together.

Soon there were hundreds of us with our overloaded carts, rumbling toward the Holy City. As we rolled and shifted our way along, I felt that I was leaving my grief behind, and my loneliness. As a farewell gift from my husband, I could hear him assuring me that I would not be free to make this journey if he were still alive.

Passing near Mount Ebal, we spent an extra day to take advantage of the stream that was full and generous in spring. We women sat together at midday, sharing our bread and dried fruit.

It was the first time I regretted leaving Phineas behind in Sepphoris. I had no servants to send ahead of me. I wanted to let Claudia Procula know that I would be in Jerusalem and hoped to see her. I mentioned this to my cousin, as it was on my mind. She nodded her head to show that she heard my wish, but offered no suggestions.

As we lingered over our modest meal, we could see a man riding into camp on horseback, followed by two servants. His stallion's shining coat and his own fine woolen robe announced that he was a man of privilege.

"Joseph, the spice trader," a woman beside me whispered to me. We all knew soon enough, the distinguished member of the Jewish Council and an admirer of my cousin was in our company.

She kept to herself, straightening her robe with brisk flicks of her hands. Joses, the gentle one, soon came for her. Mary rose without looking in our direction, reached for the young man's hand and went with him to receive her caller. The giggling and nodding grew louder among us, until my cousin returned and motioned for me to follow her.

"We will tell him you have a message to be delivered," she said.

I could see Joseph in the clearing ahead of us, his round face shining in the sun. I walked a few steps in front of my cousin with her mild, well-mannered escort ahead of me. We made it difficult for my cousin's visitor to catch sight of her too soon.

He spoke to me first, looking past me for a glimpse of Mary.

"Joanna," he said, "blessings upon you." Then, with more consideration, he added, "Your husband was a good man."

He explained to Joses, but in a voice so that we all could hear, how he was on his way home to Jerusalem from Armenia with a shipment he planned to sell during the festival. Some miles behind him on the road, he said, he noticed our caravan coming from the north. He guessed it might include the teacher's family.

His men went ahead while he rode back, half a day's hard ride, hoping to see "faithful friends," as he put it. He smoothed his hair, a half-moon of dark fur that framed his large head.

My cousin was a bit more reserved than usual, but her smile made up for it. Joseph's brown cheeks brightened. "Dear lady," he said, beaming with admiration. "You must be wondering how I found your campsite. Let me say, I can be very determined."

Forgetting his manners, he let his gaze linger on her. She allowed him this indulgence, but only briefly.

"Joseph," she said, "won't you come and sit in the shade?" She led him toward a sycamore, glancing in my direction as she passed me, silently advising that I stay close.

The scent of wild dill drifted near the wall where Joseph leaned his back. He faced my cousin and soon was lost in her gentle eyes and the silver strands that grew more noticeable by the month in her black hair. I could see how much he cared for her.

I wanted to give them their privacy and so offered to bring them water. I took my time returning. By then they were well along in conversation.

"I gave them each a name," my cousin was saying as I placed the water jug near her.

"The cows?" Joseph chuckled. His rich man's belly shook with delight.

"They are Barley and Custard, to match their colors," she said.

My cousin and her caller were discreet as they basked in each other's company. Stepping back, I tried once again to leave them alone.

Another burst of enthusiasm from Joseph changed my plan. "Joanna, come and sit beside your cousin," he insisted, making room for me. With Mary near him, he was more outgoing than I had ever seen him.

Calling one of his servants, he sent the man to bring a certain package from his luggage. The servant returned with a large pouch bound up by a silk cord. My cousin carefully opened it and lifted a shawl of midnight-blue embroidered with golden nightingales, from Joseph's travels in Asia. We admired the needlework, and Mary wrapped the luxurious fabric around her shoulders but soon put it aside. Nothing could distract her from her guest.

In the midst of his affectionate glances, I thought of Manaen, who often looked at Mary with his own sort of appreciation. Near her he turned into warm honey. How had I missed it? Two such powerful men were completely taken by my cousin's ways. From the time they met Mary, neither one had let her out of his sight for long.

"My servant will stay with you," Joseph was saying. "Send him immediately to me if there is anything you need."

"There is something," she said. "My cousin Joanna has a message to be delivered."

Joseph listened without so much as turning toward me, preferring to smile happily at her. Mary explained that I hoped to get word to the governor's wife, telling her when I would arrive in Jerusalem.

"Let me take care of it," Joseph said, beaming just to think that he could do something more to please my cousin. "I have done business with the governor's wife many times in the past. I will send word to her when I am in Jerusalem, three days from now. I have cinnabar and jade from my travels. She is always interested. When I see her I will deliver your message myself."

He was too subtle a man to remind us that he often met with the governor, as well. The same thought must have come to Mary.

"My son may arrive in Jerusalem before us," she said.

Joseph looked at her attentively. An understanding passed between them.

"Perhaps he will honor me and stay at my house," Joseph said.

He left us the next morning. My cousin seemed in better spirits than she had been for some weeks. A strong feeling came over me that his visit would be the most carefree time of our journey.

We continued south. At each town we gathered the news of the area. Near Sychar, we heard that my healer had passed that way six days before us. When residents of the village learned that he was on his way to the Hebrew festival, they refused to allow him to enter their gate, although he had taught the crowds and healed their sick in the past.

Near Corea we heard that the teacher was speaking to the crowds when a man asked if he was the Anointed One, who would save the Hebrews from their oppressors. When he answered that yes, he was sent by the Almighty, some laughed at him, but many more threw stones. He made more new enemies that day.

By the time we reached Bethphage, two miles outside Jerusalem, a number of us were concerned about my healer. Simon came to Mary and said he would ride to Bethany, a short distance away. The teacher often stayed there at the house of his friends, Lazarus and his sisters. Simon would ask his brother to wait for the family so that they could enter Jerusalem together.

The day Simon returned to us, I was with my cousin in the tent of a woman who had gone into labor. She was so frightened that Mary had to remind her to breathe. I rubbed the young mother's cold blue feet.

I heard Simon outside. Mary went out to meet him. I could hear them talking.

"I have seen my brother," Simon began.

"Where is he?" Mary asked.

"At the house of his friends."

In what I mistook, at first, for a muffled laugh, Simon began to weep. I went to the entrance of the tent, where I could see Mary putting her arms around him. He pressed his face against her shoulder but still could not stop his tears.

"Simon," she said at last. "What happened?"

"He has raised a man from the dead. Lazarus had been buried for four days."

I could hardly take it in. My own awe and terror were mirrored in my cousin's face. I wished I could hear what prayers she was saying in her silence. Maybe then I would know whether to give thanks for the miracle of a dead man returned to life, or to beg for the life of the one who saved him.

Simon took Mary's hands and leaned toward her. A rough man, awkward by nature, he spoke in a low voice that was his way of showing his concern for her.

"People ran to my brother and knelt down to worship him."

"Did you speak to him?"

"I asked him to come back here and stay close to us. He said he was going into the city."

Many among us sat by the campfire through that night. It was quite late when I went to see about my cousin. She had gone off on her own, hours earlier. I found her in an open field. Believing that no one could hear her, she stood facing heaven, speaking her thoughts out loud. It was a cry of such anguish it stopped me from going closer.

"If you knew it would end this way, why did you include me?" Her voice was low and rasping, a parched sound. "A man like him should be born of a mountain, not a woman. I am not strong enough for him. Please, listen to me. I am not that strong."

I had to turn away. I could not look at her.

The stars seemed indifferent. I imagined how they lit the white stones of the temple courtyard and equally so the frightened animals that would be slaughtered there. It was three days before Passover, the feast of liberation.

CHAPTER THIRTEEN

...his wife sent word to him, "Have nothing to do with that innocent man, for today I have suffered a great deal because of a dream about him."

—*Matthew* 27:19

As we approached the feast day, my cousin did not brood over her worries but joined the rest of us in our preparations. At night, there were stories about the first Passover and the pillarlike cloud that crossed the sky guiding the Hebrews through the desert to freedom.

I listened and understood that one equally as mysterious was leading me into my future. I might never have followed, if my own freedom of a sort had not been imposed on me. Soon after my husband's death I became an exile. I was not welcome in the powerful circles where I once moved. Except for Procula, my so-called friends at court no longer invited me.

It was a strange sensation to be buried alive and left for dead. Overnight, I was reduced to a mere ghost of my former self, hovering between two worlds, no longer welcome in one, not certain where I fit in the other.

One morning as I woke from a deep sleep, I caught a glimpse of what lay ahead for me, although I did not know its meaning. I heard the sound of a quiet voice calling to me from the edge of my dreams.

"Joanna," I heard. "Go to Nazareth."

I puzzled over the words. Why would I do such a thing when my cousin Mary was with me on the road to Jerusalem? I had no answer, and so I followed the example of my servant, Phineas. When he did not fully understand an order, he waited in silence for further instructions.

On the day before Passover, we plucked and peeled and scrubbed for the feast. It was my introduction to the preparations. I was like a child trying to follow the grown-ups as I attempted the most basic chores. One of my jobs was to mash the hyssop to a pulp, and then the marjoram. Grinding the wheat, I sent specks of grain flying like dust from the stone. I quickly plucked them out of the dirt, hoping no one noticed.

Through the morning, a white glare settled over us and held the heat close upon us. No sunshine managed to break through. I had expected cooler weather in the foothills, but the willows and aspens rarely stirred to suggest the start of a breeze. It was an unusual display of nature's bad temper.

We continued our work and watched for a break in the clouds.

I went on to my next task, scrubbing cups and polishing them with a clean cloth. It was my best achievement, except that I did not know what prayers to say as I cleaned. I worried that the drinking cups would not be as pure without the holy words. The devout women who busied themselves around me could have told me what to pray, but in truth I was too proud to ask.

When I had finished all of my work, I brought my cousin the basket of grain that I had prepared. She picked out the pebbles and bits of dirt, absentmindedly tossing them aside as if she were straightening a child's braid.

"I wonder if my son will join us," she said.

I started to correct her. Mary knew as I did that he had already entered Jerusalem. He certainly would not leave there. His enemies would call him a coward.

"He has surprised me in the past," she said.

At the sound of the shofar, our companions began to gather together and say the prayers. We joined them. My cousin's watchful eyes told me she had not given up her wish. As night came, the sky cleared. A bright full moon encouraged us to linger near the fire. The Passover moon, lighting the way as it had the night the Israelites escaped from slavery.

Some among us told stories about the desert, where water gushed from a stone and the droppings of insects were the ancestor's daily food. I tried to imagine my own relatives among the ancient ones. Did any of them consider that one day a daughter would be cut off from the Hebrews and rejected by the conquerors she had befriended? How well I now fit among the outcasts and outsiders who followed Jesus.

I was stirred from my bleak recollection by the sound of horses and unfriendly voices that reached us from the valley below us. Some of the men in our group went to secure the animals. Mothers lifted their young ones, asleep in their arms, and hurried away. I had always heard about the Roman invasions of the pilgrims' camps. The riots that broke out at such times used to exhaust my husband, whose job it was to control them.

An eager young man stood up and uncovered his knife. Others filled their pockets with rocks and followed him. We heard shouting and heavy footsteps not far from us. Hardly any time passed before I could see by the bright moon that Roman soldiers were chasing our men back up the hill from the valley.

I stood on the edge of a cart for a better view. The soldiers charged, until all at once their leader pulled ahead of them and slowed their speed by stretching out his arms and lowering his hands toward the ground.

I strained to see his face as I vaguely recognized his gestures. Was it Chuza who disciplined his men in that way? I could not recall.

Three soldiers rode toward us. The others stayed at a distance, alert to any change. The women sitting near me scrambled to hide. Some of the men picked up cooking pots or tree branches for weapons.

I was unable to move in my terror and soon could see the leader more clearly. He walked a few steps ahead of the others, with his head facing downward toward the rugged path. He was so close I could hear the groan of his armor.

I hurried to my cousin, who stood motionless, frightened as I was. We listened to the soldiers riding into our camp. The older men, those who had stayed behind with us women, formed a wall in front of us, a last attempt to protect their property. I heard a clear command from the other side.

"Get back, we don't want to hurt anyone."

I recognized the voice and went toward it, stopping to be sure. All at once I saw Manaen, attracting all the moonlight.

I fell into his arms in unspeakable relief. We were safe. I knew it.

"Joanna," he said, with such emotion that it startled me. I stepped back and looked at him. I had not realized how much I missed him.

"My cousin Mary is with me."

"I know."

"How did you find us?"

"Joseph, the spice dealer."

If I had once imagined myself to be clever at recognizing the worthy and the undeserving, Manaen's answer showed me that I was not wise. Joseph the spy, his mission to keep watch over the innocent. I never suspected. The world is a far more subtle and complex place than I gave it credit for. There in Bethphage on the first night of Passover I discovered this. It was a blessing of the feast.

When he saw my cousin, Manaen went to her. Bending toward her, he spoke so as not to be overheard. I went and stood near them.

"Your son has been arrested," he said. "Some of the religious leaders have taken him to Caiphas."

"Where is he?" she urged. "Please, take me to him." Mary set out toward the darkness. Manaen stepped in front of her and signaled two soldiers. "We are taking this woman to Jerusalem," he said.

One of them went into the night and returned with a horse and cart. Obviously, Manaen had planned everything. He came to lead my cousin out of danger. All the rest, the noisy approach, the threats, the invasion, was for show.

Mary's neighbors and relatives stood watching but did not try to defend her. It was clear that she wanted to go with the soldiers. One of Manaen's men helped her into the cart. I dared to speak out. "My cousin will be safer if I am with her."

Manaen was close enough so that he could answer without being overheard. He told me that he would take Mary to a certain house in Jerusalem. It belonged to a teacher of the law who followed Jesus, but in secret. No one would look for her there.

"Pilate's wife expects me," I persisted. "Claudia Procula can help my healer. Let me bring his mother to her. She will see that my cousin's son is from a good family."

Manaen looked to Mary. Her eyes were bright pools lit by her terror.

Manaen did not answer me, but only helped me into the cart beside my cousin. We rode quickly toward the city. I used our time alone to explain my plan to her. I knew that she would not argue with me, for fear of unwanted attention.

"We must both go to Claudia Procula," I said. "When she meets you, she will understand."

"Her husband hates my people," Mary answered.

"Claudia Procula can go to Pilate," I insisted. "She can tell him that Jesus is a holy man. It will go better for him if you talk to her."

To save her son, Mary fell silent.

We rode toward the Damascus gate. Manaen dropped back as we were about enter the city and motioned our escort to stop. He rode up beside us, took hold of the reins and steadied our horses.

"The house is just ahead," he told my cousin.

Her answer surprised me, as she had not spoken to me for most of our time alone. "It is best for my son if I go with Joanna and talk to the governor's wife," she said.

Manaen shook his head to disagree.

"No one will look for her there," I said. In my eagerness I tripped over the words. He leaned closer, to hear me. His sudden nearness confused me all the more. I stopped, unable to say anything at all.

He looked at me as if he noticed something about me he had never seen before. He was surprised, as I was, by our exchange. He slowly leaned away.

"Please," Mary said. "It has to be this way."

Manaen gave up arguing. "As you say."

* * *

We rode to the Roman quarter. At the palace, Manaen spoke to the guards and ordered two of his men to escort us to Claudia Procula's apartment. Before he left us, he assured my cousin that he would help her son. He promised to send her word as soon as he had news of the teacher.

It was the fourth watch, not yet daybreak. The lights burned hot in Claudia Procula's rooms. She opened the door, and I stepped back at the sight of her. She was dressed in a sleeping gown. Her hair was loose and tangled. When she embraced me, I smelled wine.

"I'm not well," she said. "My astrologer, Darius, has been here. I have been troubled ever since." She looked at my cousin with suspicion. A weak smile crossed her lips.

"Darius said I would have a visitor tonight. I hoped it would be you, Joanna," she said. Turning her back to Mary, she scolded me. "He didn't say there would be two women."

"This is my cousin, the mother of my healer," I began.

"Yes, of course," Procula interrupted me. Another half smile moved across her lips as she walked away from us and went to lie down on her couch. "Joanna, my pet, have something to drink," she said, waving a command toward her maidservant, who sat by the door. "Bring some glasses," she ordered the girl.

"The mother of my healer," I tried again. Procula took a long sip from her cup. I doubt she heard me.

"You must be very tired," she sighed toward Mary. "Let my servants show you your room. You should try to sleep."

"I am here because of my son," Mary said. She had no intention of leaving us.

"Is something wrong?" Procula asked. Her voice hardened. "Joanna?"

I stood between the two women, prepared for Mary to walk defiantly out of the house. She watched us as she made her decision. I could almost hear her, considering her son's best interests. She stood quietly near the door. I asked Claudia Procula to excuse us and I accompanied Mary to her room.

"She doesn't know what has happened," Mary said impatiently as we followed the servants along the hallway. "You have to make her understand."

"I need a little time," I said. "Let me talk to her alone. Pilate will not decide anything tonight."

I left my cousin and hurried back along the corridor. Claudia Procula stood waiting for me with a cup of wine in her hand.

"Jo-aaanna," she sang sweetly. "Drink this. You'll feel better. I can't tell you how happy it makes me, seeing you."

Her waxen skin told me she had been wrestling with nightmares. Her robe was now falling open. Barefoot, hardly able to hold her silver cup, she went to the window and watched the moon as it dropped low in the sky. "We will be all alone," she moaned.

"My healer, Jesus the Nazarene, he has been arrested," I said, ignoring the cup she waved at me until she put it down.

"My astrologer told me there would be a terrible disturbance of nature tonight." She pushed her tangled mane back from her forehead and called me to her side.

"Stay with me while I sleep," she said, clutching my hand. We stumbled back to her couch and she lay down. "I am so frightened."

I could not allow her to sleep. "My healer, Jesus, the one I have told you about, needs your help," I said.

"What has he done?" She lay back as if it was an effort to stay awake.

"So many now follow him that his enemies fear he will divide his people."

"Darius told me," Claudia Procula said, slurring the words. "The gods will play a trick on my Pilate. They will send him one of their own in disguise." She gripped my hand and sat up. Her teeth began to chatter as if she had caught a chill.

"I have to warn my husband. Help me. What should I tell him?"

With all the force in me I took hold of her moist arms and held her steady. I was not certain that she could hear me.

"Tell Pilate he must not harm this holy man."

She fell back on her couch, tossing one arm over her eyes. "The gods have turned against us," she whimpered, until she slipped into fitful sleep.

Through the window, I watched black fingers slide across the moon like the dangerous reach of an assassin. Only a few fingers at first, then an invasion that choked the light. What had been a perfect pearl in the sky was now hacked and marred. The angel of death was passing over us. I closed my eyes, too frightened to watch.

From the table beside Claudia Procula, I took the rinse cloth from the basin and pressed it against her cheeks. The coolness of the water brought her back from sleep. She sat up, twisted to see behind her, leaped up and went toward the window. "It's not his fault!" she shrieked to the heavens.

Without the moonlight, the room was now dark. I groped for the candle, lit it and went toward her, speaking her name repeatedly, only to reassure her. Her eyes gleamed. She was a frightened doe who backed away from me, expecting me to harm her.

"The king of the Jews is nailed to a Roman cross," she shrieked. She was trying to make me understand.

"No," I said. "There isn't any king. You were dreaming."

"My husband." She turned her face upward and watched her dream play itself out along the pale expanse. "Pilate poured blood on the ground. When he turned to show me, his mouth was full of fire."

I tried to hold her, to keep her from clawing at herself. "The floor beneath him was torn open," she gasped. "My husband fell. No one could save him." Her hand swung wildly. Her fingernails ripped my cheek. "Blood like rain," she screamed. "The house of Caesar is smeared with blood."

She backed away from me, sobbing. "I am drowning in blood."

At last, servants and guards rushed into the room. My tortured friend pointed to one of the servants and issued a command. "Go to my husband," she said, her hands fluttering around her ears. "Tell him I have suffered dreams. Say that he must have nothing to do with the Nazarene." She threw off the maidservant, who was trying to hold her still.

"I'll go to him, myself!" she shouted. She ran, but the guards stepped into her path. Their touch on her fragile body prevented her. One of the guards placed her limp figure on her couch.

My cousin was among the servants gathered at the door who witnessed this sight. Mary's half-closed eyes told me that she had made up her mind about our disappointing ally. Procula was not capable of doing more than sending her husband a warning. Tears burned my eyes. Mary showed no such signs of defeat.

"Joanna," she said. I followed her in swift silence through the corridor and down the steps. On the lower level of the house, when the iron gate was almost in reach, a guard the size of a bull entered from the street. The dawn sky was the color of a dove's breast.

The guard came toward me with purpose. I expected him to arrest us, but instead he asked for my cousin, calling her Mary the Nazarene.

"I am the one you are looking for," she said. She was expectant, as if she knew he would come.

"My captain, Manaen, sends word," he said. "I am to tell you that Jesus, the teacher from Galilee, has been charged with blasphemy by the religious leaders."

My cousin listened, slowly sinking as if she would fall, but she did not take her eyes from the guard's face.

"Where is my son?" she asked.

"At the governor's headquarters."

Mary started for the heavy gate while the guard continued his account. She stood with one hand pressed against the bars that separated us from the street.

"The governor met with the religious council," the messenger said.

Joseph the spice merchant was in that room, although the guard did not mention him.

"All but two voted against the Galilean."

"Those who voted against him," I asked, unable to control my obsession with details, "what punishment did they call for?"

The guard did not answer.

Mary pushed with all her strength to open the gate. I followed her into the street. The moon was a faded disk, so sheer that I could almost see through it.

The guard was close behind me, shouting that we were to follow him. He was to take us out of Jerusalem. I did not pause but expected him to stop me by force, which he did not. We could see my cousin ahead of us, rushing along the street, her veil waving like a banner leading a charge.

I stumbled once, not by accident. The hem of my robe caught on a briar bush, which slowed us down once more. We arrived at the governor's headquarters not far behind my cousin. She turned suddenly to face us, and the guard stopped midstep. I urged him to leave us. "I will stay with her," I said.

From then on he followed us closely, but he did not speak to us again, nor did he try to direct our course.

CHAPTER FOURTEEN

"When Herod saw Jesus he was very glad, for he had been wanting to see him for a long time, because he had heard about him and was hoping to see him perform some sign."

—*Luke* 23:8

In the courtyard next to the governor's palace, Pilate listened to testimony about my healer while Jesus stood before him. The street outside boiled with commotion. Strangers leaned into one another's faces demanding to know what the outcome of the hearing might be. Only the first to arrive at the palace were allowed to enter the yard. It soon overflowed so that most of the crowd was forced to wait outside the wall.

We expected that one of Pilate's men would come out to us and announce a verdict, innocent or guilty. We were not prepared for what happened instead. A mob rushed from the building, shouting the results of the hearing. Pilate had refused to pass judgment for or against Jesus. Instead, he ordered that my healer be led to Herod Antipas for questioning.

"The prophet from Galilee should be judged by the Tetrarch of Galilee," someone from the mob shouted above the din. I stopped an old man wobbling toward me. I recognized him from long ago. It was Zorah, the cripple whom Jesus healed in Capernaum.

"Pilate said Jesus is innocent," Zorah assured me in his thin voice.

I took his arm, trying to slow him down. "Where are they taking him now?" I asked.

"Pilate couldn't find any crime to charge him with."

"But did he release Jesus?" I persisted.

"A messenger came into the courtyard while Asa was defending the healer. He had cured Asa of his blindness."

I tried to hurry Zorah along. "What did the messenger say?"

"We could not hear him. But when he left, Pilate ended the hearing. He only said that he saw no reason to convict Jesus."

"Procula," I breathed. Claudia Procula's warning must have reached the governor. Pilate didn't dare to pass judgment when he heard of his wife's ominous dream, but he didn't release Jesus, either. Something in him could not allow Pilate to free a Hebrew. Not any Hebrew. He hated them all, as much as they hated him.

All around me, a wild herd pounded its way toward Antipas's chambers. Mary and I got caught in the stampede and were carried along to the place where Jesus was going to be questioned.

My demented tetrarch was finally getting his way. After insisting for months that I arrange a meeting, after poisoning my husband in part because he failed to bring my healer to Tiberias, Antipas was about to have his wish to meet Jesus granted. Pilate himself had arranged it. Pilate, who loathed Antipas and would never do anything for him if he could help it.

Once I knew where we were going, I pushed and elbowed ahead, arm in arm with Mary, so that we would be among the first to reach the place and would see with our own eyes.

In my determination I put aside fear. I was running toward my enemy, who might very well kill me if he found me in his reach. Good, I told myself, I will die with the man who once saved me from death. It was enough for me.

"I'm going alone from here," my cousin suddenly announced. Her arm was outstretched in front of me to bar my way. "It's too dangerous for you."

She kept moving but seemed to expect me to stop and fall behind. I kept pace with her, however.

"I know how to talk to Antipas," I said. "I can try to convince him."

We had not spoken more than a few words all morning, sparing each other our worries. Now, once again, we fell silent, each waiting for the other to say something. I couldn't promise Mary that I would persuade Antipas, but she must have understood, as I did, that we needed to take care of each other.

"All right, then," she answered. I raised the scarf from my shoulders and covered my head as we hurried to the tetrarch's gate. The mob was trying to push past the guards, who swung their clubs and whips at them. I managed to squirm free, holding on to Mary. There was a side entrance into the property where my own servants once came and went. It was surely the gate that Octavia entered the night she betrayed my husband. At that early hour of the morning, the only guard posted there was dozing. We slipped past him.

Mary kept a brisk pace as we dashed up a flight of stairs to the second-floor arcade. We stepped into a small room with a clear view of the main interior courtyard below us. We watched as six guards posted themselves around the yard. Two servants entered, carrying Antipas's chair to the elevated walkway above the stone paved yard. From there the tetrarch could look down on everyone.

When the royal chair was put in plain sight before us, my cousin turned to examine my face without asking any question. She must have seen that I was determined to stay.

A few men from the Hebrew council who had come to accuse Jesus entered the yard and stood close to the empty chair. Soon after that my healer was led across the stone floor to the stand facing them. At the sight of her son, Mary took a sudden breath, not loud, but it startled me. I stepped back, and my foot touched a lamp stand I had not even noticed earlier.

"We can't make any sound," I whispered to her.

As Antipas came into the courtyard, I pulled my scarf close around my face. I had lived in fear of seeing him again. I could only hope that no one would come along the hallway and discover us.

Antipas went straight to Jesus, excited by the beaten figure before him. He smiled smugly, confident that he had out-smarted a shrewd opponent. Pacing, watching, he jabbed the air to test for a reaction. My healer did not move.

"So this is Jesus of Nazareth." He spoke to the council, as well as to his guards and servants—a small audience, but he made use of it. "I've heard so much about this prophet from Nazareth. The miracle worker, isn't that what they call you?"

He untied my healer's hands and turned his back to him. "Go on, work a miracle. Save yourself."

Antipas walked away, turned abruptly and came back.

"Tell me, prophet," he said, "what is my future?"

What else would a man intoxicated with himself want to know?

"My soothsayer tells me I will be remembered through all of history," Antipas confidently assured his audience. Then, less confidently, he spoke again to Jesus. "But he can't tell me why. You tell me."

My healer shook his head no, just slightly. The tetrarch seized on the gesture.

"No? Surely you don't mean there is no future for Antipas."
He began to laugh like a neighing horse.

"I order you. Tell me how I will be remembered." His own
hopes for the future suddenly tumbled from his lips. "I am to
be governor of Jerusalem—isn't that it?"

The anger building inside of Antipas frightened me. I
knew what he was capable of when he felt threatened or
confused.

"Answer me or you'll hang."

I must have stepped back without thinking. The lamp
behind me dove from its pedestal and smashed on the floor.

In the awful stillness, Antipas looked up toward the room
where we hid. Three guards were already on the stairs.

"Stay here," I said, urging Mary deeper into the room.

She did not argue. It was her way to let me try my own
plan first. She would let me go to meet Antipas, just as she
let me call upon Procula only hours earlier. If I failed now,
as before, she would take action on her own. But not until
she gave me my chance. Her trust in me made me all the
more determined.

I stepped out of the room and met the guards head-on.
They had me locked in their iron fists before I could protest.
I did not give up easily. I wanted Antipas to see me before
they dragged me away. Each was as strong as an ox. There was
no getting around them.

"Take your hands off me!" I shouted in a last attempt to
maintain my dignity. "I am Joanna, widow of Chuza, Herod
Antipas's chief steward. How dare you touch me!"

The scene I was part of froze. All of us were set in granite before my eyes, turned into an artist's rendition. No one moved for what felt to me like many hours.

"Wait," Antipas commanded. "Bring her here."

Convinced that it was the hour of my death, I had no need for caution. I looked with defiance at my guards until they let me go. Walking down the stairs as if I were entering my own throne room, I crossed the courtyard.

I went to my healer and I knelt down before him. I took his crusted hand and pressed it to my lips. I could feel how death had settled over him. He was at peace with it. I lifted my face to him and saw compassion, thinly veiled by an unfamiliar distance. He was among us but no longer one of us. He had prepared himself for the worst.

"No," I pleaded with him, pressing his hand against my cheek. "Not like this."

"Joanna." Antipas's voice split the air. "Well, well, Joanna."

I turned, still on my knees.

"At last. Here we all are," he said. "You and me and your miracle worker, together. What a pity that your husband isn't with us. My fallen comrade, Chuza."

Without rising, I spoke to him. "I heard you say that you will be governor," I began, falsely confident. "I know what you want. I can help you. I have friends, people with influence."

"Oh, really?" he answered, amused more than anything. "And who are these friends of yours?"

"My husband was highly regarded by Lucius Vitellius. It is expected that he will be the next governor of Syria. What he commands is what will be. I can send word to him and tell him all the things that my husband said in praise of you."

"He doesn't care about the opinions of some foolish woman."

"Claudia Procula." I rushed headlong, making promises. "She is my loyal friend. I know she will speak to her husband, the governor, on your behalf if I ask her."

Antipas nodded his head, an exaggerated wag, making fun of me to his audience.

"And what do you want in return for these favors you're offering?" he asked, looking out at his guards to let them in on the joke.

"Set this innocent man free."

The room burst into laughter.

Antipas turned his back to us and walked away. The threat of violence weighed the air. I could hardly breathe.

"Now, now, Joanna," he said. "Please, stand up. My loyal steward's widow, you don't have to kneel for your tetrarch." He took my arm and led me to one side. "There, now, you can see everything from here," he said. He turned back to Jesus.

"I have heard that you say Jerusalem's temple is going to be destroyed," he began. "No stone will be left on another stone. So then, prophet, it is your own people who will suffer, not the allies of Rome. Isn't that what you said?"

Antipas walked over to the councilmen to be certain they were paying attention. "Tell me, prophet, how long will my kingdom last?"

He jabbed my healer's chest, but Jesus refused to speak. His strong silence unnerved Antipas.

"Listen to me!" Antipas shouted to the room. "I'm warning you. This man plans to attack the city."

He stopped pacing and looked carefully at the clotted hair and stained face. "You understand, prophet," he said, "we can't have you threatening my subjects this way. You could start a riot."

Antipas looked again for approval from the council. His features sharpened. The fox was circling his prey.

"And when the temple is destroyed, what then? Maybe you'd like to be king of the Jews, is that your plan?"

He laughed at his own cleverness. "You see, Joanna, you might be back at court before you know it. Your healer wants to be a king."

Spinning on his heel, Antipas went to the servant, who held his cloak, pulled it into his own hands and came striding toward Jesus.

"A king needs a proper wardrobe," he said. He shook open the heavy linen cloak and wrapped it around Jesus, fastening the silver pin at the neckline. Then he turned my healer around to face the guards and servants in the yard.

"Bow down to the King," he commanded.

The council members stood firm, nervously refusing to move. But the guards fell to their knees as if Caesar was passing by. Some of them rolled over onto the ground, braying like mules. I waited for my healer to defend himself, but he said nothing.

Antipas looked from his guards to the expectant faces of the council, to be sure that everyone was watching. He raised his thumb slowly into the air, held it high and brought it down in a swift motion. "Take him to Pilate," he said. "I leave the last word to the governor."

Mary stepped into the doorway of the upper room and looked down at her son intently, but she did not call out. It was enough for her that he saw her and knew she was with him.

The tetrarch did not notice their exchange. He was watching the freak show going on among the guards, his eyes dancing with pleasure.

"Your healer is a foolish man, Joanna," he called to me. "He saved your life, but not his own." Pulling the robe off of Jesus, he whipped it into the air for a servant to catch.

"Burn this," he said with contempt. Then he motioned his guards to take Jesus away. I was about to go with him.

"Not you, Joanna," Antipas said. I stopped, knowing that I was about to be arrested.

He let me dangle in front of him while he considered which punishment would cause me the greatest pain. As always in such matters, he made the best choice.

"Go watch him die," he said, waving a hand to dismiss me.

I remained, trembling, unable to walk. When I gathered myself together at last, the courtyard was empty. I went to the stairs to find my cousin. She was standing like a shadow just inside the door to the upper room. She came soundlessly down the stairs.

We left there and went back to Pilate's quarters, where we were forced to crowd together with men and women who had lost their reason. Whining, snarling like hyenas, they were not able to tell their friends from their enemies.

The governor made quick work of the final verdict. He let the crowd decide.

The chanting began. "Crucify him."

I believe they had Antipas in their heart, not my healer, as they railed. But it was Jesus they pointed to in their rage.

CHAPTER FIFTEEN

"But all his acquaintances, including some women who had followed him from Galilee, stood at a distance, watching these things."

—*Luke* 23:49

My healer was led to the Place of Skulls, where they killed him.

I followed, memories floating past me, some bursting open before my eyes. He drank and danced with us. He taught us to see the world around us as never before. The poor are rich, a field lily is more splendid than a king's robes.

He went easily from the company of scholars and lawyers to the straw mats of homeless cripples, and dined with tax collectors who worked for Caesar, and befriended shameless women. He met all of us where he found us and led us onward from there. For this, he aroused suspicion that simmered and turned to hate.

What lesson was I to draw from this example? An honorable life is an act of courage.

Mary and I stayed close by him, along with a few others who were with us. I recognized Hannah, the woman who gave Jesus a home in Capernaum. Zorah, of course, was on the hill. I also saw several of my cousin's neighbors from Nazareth. And there was one woman I recognized from the first time I saw my healer. Mary of Magdala, who was with Jesus in Capernaum the day that I went to the market there to shop for spices and trinkets.

I remembered how she took my hand and tried to lead me to my healer. I thought again of how she frightened me and how I ran away. Would it have changed anything if I had allowed her to help me that day? My willfulness has been such a costly flaw.

We women stayed together as we climbed the hill following behind the man we loved. All along the way the rocky hilltop threatened. Not the hill itself but the wooden posts that stood upright in the stones, waiting for their next victims.

It was close to midday, but the sun had refused to come out from behind the clouds. A gray light released a soft drizzle upon us. I stewed in morbid thoughts. If only the soldiers would tie my healer to the post, not pound iron spikes into him. Rope his arms to a crossbeam and leave him that way—it would be less painful than nailing his hands and feet to the wood.

If there had to be nails, I wanted to choose them. Frugal Pilate had ordered that they be pried from one corpse and hammered into the next man. The spikes for my healer's bones should come from the hands and feet of a holy man, like him. These hopeless dreams beat against the walls of my head.

I would have preferred avoiding a close look at Jesus, but his mother wanted to be as near to her son as she could manage. We were within reach of him when he collapsed. Mary would have run to him, but a young man was suddenly at her side, speaking only to her.

I knew him to be one of the teacher's closest followers. Mary answered him, calling him by his name, John. He was very gentle with her and stood modestly beside her without trying to manage things. They were together from then on. I could see how he calmed her.

More than halfway up the hill, I still had not seen any of the other twelve. Where were they? I wondered if they might have gone ahead, to bribe the soldiers at the top of the hill to release their beloved teacher.

The truth is, there were many more of us who had been cured of our diseases than there were family or friends on that path. I kept to myself, lost in panic and confusion. At any moment, I told myself, the Almighty will send the angels to throw off the guards and cast them to the ground.

I listened for the beating of blessed wings. But I heard the place of death calling. "Bring here your rebels and traitors and all who fall out of favor with Jerusalem's leaders," the hilltop beckoned through blackening clouds.

Close to the end of our climb, a soldier pushed my healer to hurry him along. The crossbeam rolled off his shoulder and he fell. Mary reached for him, shouting, "Let him go." One of the guards pulled a wooden club from his belt and swung it at her.

"Kill me, don't kill my son!" she shrieked.

Some of the other women began pounding their chests in sympathy. Old Hannah threw stones at the soldiers until someone near her held her back to keep her from getting whipped to death.

When we reached our destination, nothing could mask the smell of rotting flesh. I had never been to the Place of Skulls, but even to pass by from below required covering my face with my scarf to block out the foul odor.

At times there were twenty or even fifty bodies hanging on the posts. Some of the dying had the bad fortune to suffer for days.

My cousin and I stood with young John and Mary the Magdalene, Hannah and a few of the other women of Galilee. The sound of death cut through the stormy air. Nails pounding into flesh; groaning, sudden gasping from pain filled our ears. I stood beside Mary, determined to be strong for her until at last it was over.

He died quickly. In truth none of us was prepared. We expected to be with him in his agony for hours, perhaps days. My eyes were cast down to the ground as I considered all that should be arranged for a decent burial. None of it had been done, and I could not think who among us had the strength to bury him now. So little time was left before sundown and the start of the Sabbath. After that it would be impossible to arrange anything until the next evening.

My eyes searched the rough ground for an answer, and it came to me in the form of a fine linen robe. I first recognized Joseph the spice merchant by the hem of his garment. He was standing in front of me. My cousin looked at him, and fresh tears filled her eyes.

"I will take care of everything," he said to her.

My cousin leaned against him, just for a moment. "Joanna," she said. "Go with Joseph. He will need your help."

I could not move. Young John and the women who were with us circled closer around Mary. I watched them but did not react.

"Joanna," my cousin called to me. "There isn't much time." Without answering her, I did as she asked and followed Joseph down the hill.

CHAPTER SIXTEEN

"Now there was a good and righteous man named Joseph who…went to Pilate and asked for the body of Jesus. Then he took it down, wrapped it in linen cloth, and laid it in a rock-hewn tomb where no one had ever been laid."

—*Luke* 23:50,52-53

Joseph's cart and driver were waiting at the foot of the hill. We went first to the stonecutter's workshop near the Hebrew cemetery. As we rode the short distance he sat in the front seat beside his driver, and I was behind them. But Joseph turned sideways, rather than put his back toward me.

For a time we were caught up in our separate concerns. Although it was dark, we had almost two hours before the start of the Sabbath. I could not see how we would find a tomb, prepare a body and hold a proper burial. Joseph seemed to understand.

"Joanna," he said, his face pressed closer to me. He must have been speaking to me for some time, although I had not heard him.

"Yes," I said, sitting straighter than before.

"We have a tomb," he began. "We will go to the stonecutter and settle the details."

"We can't bury him in the paupers' field," I insisted. "Isn't there some way you can arrange for him to lie in the Hebrew cemetery?"

I knew it was against the law. A man condemned as a criminal was forbidden to rest with the holy ancestors.

We entered beneath the stonecutter's sign into a yard where men sharpened and repaired mallets and picks, their arms and faces powdered with flying dust. I followed Joseph to a small hut and entered behind him. He approached the man at the table who stood and greeted him by name.

"I am just finishing the design for the stone to cover your tomb," the man said, eager to show Joseph. The kindhearted Joseph allowed the man his proud moment, before he explained.

"There has been a change," Joseph said. "I will need the stone today."

In few words he told the cutter what he wanted the man to know.

"He is a holy prophet but not a man of worldly possessions," Joseph finished. "I will give him my own tomb. I am honored to rest his bones in my garden."

"A fine tomb for a wealthy man, why give it away?" the laborer argued. "There is another tomb I recently completed. It is in the Hebrew cemetery. The family does not need it right away. Perhaps, for a reasonable price, I can convince them."

Joseph took a large coin purse from his pocket.

"What can you arrange to cover the tomb in my garden for now?" he asked. Joseph was courteous but brief.

It was agreed that the stonecutter and his men would go to the new tomb on Joseph's property, just outside the city. They would quickly install the track that allows for the stone to be moved back and forth. There was a round stone they had cut when they began to hollow out the rock. It was still in place, and it would do.

"You are too generous, giving away the tomb that was to be your own resting place one day," the man ventured.

Joseph counted out gold pieces from his purse.

"Go to my garden and be sure that everything is arranged." Joseph spoke quickly as he was leaving. "We will bring the body within the hour."

He handed the man more than two weeks' wages. The stonecutter grasped the coins.

"We are grateful to you," Joseph said. "His mother..." He did not finish his sentence, only smiled gently at the stonecutter, who nodded in agreement.

We left there and rode into the city toward Pilate's council chambers. Several times Joseph told his driver to go faster. We stopped at the governor's gate.

"I have to speak to Pilate or at least get a message to him," Joseph said. "It will go easier for us if he gives us permission to take the body and bury it."

Once again we were reminded of my healer's disgrace. It was a Roman practice that a crucified man be punished through all eternity. Denied a proper burial, his body tossed into an open ravine beside the Place of Skulls, the dead man's spirit could never be at peace. He was doomed to eternal homelessness. Anyone who interfered by touching the body was liable to meet the same fate.

Stepping down from the cart, Joseph hesitated long enough for me to understand that he wanted to go alone.

"My cousin asked me to stay with you," I prompted him.

Any mention of Mary softened Joseph's expression. His round, moist face, usually a rosy color in her presence, was now pale as the sand. But the thought of her put the suggestion of a smile on his lips.

The idea of meeting Pilate seemed beyond my strength, but I hid my fear of him. Joseph was more decisive. Helping me down from the cart, he hurried me toward the gate.

"We have hardly more than an hour, and this is not our last stop," he said as we entered the building. I covered my face with my scarf as much as possible.

Several of the guards recognized Joseph. He asked to see the governor's first counselor. One of the guards went through a double door and returned with a low-level counselor who listened impatiently to Joseph. I stood at a distance, trying to guess the meaning of his bored expression and impatient gestures.

"Not likely," I heard the man say.

"At least ask," Joseph persisted.

Pilate's man went away. We waited for what seemed days, until the governor walked across the stone floor, by coincidence, on his way to somewhere else. He had been in one meeting and was changing rooms for another. I knew the life—Chuza's days had not been all that unlike Pilate's in some ways.

The lowly counselor, the one who spoke with Joseph earlier, now spoke to Pilate. The governor frowned as he looked across the room.

"Come," he said in his blunt manner, raising a finger in the air toward us.

Joseph approached him with confidence, whatever he might have been feeling. The governor's dull expression did not vary as he listened to the spice dealer make his request. I happened to look outside in time to see a streak of lightning thick as an iron pipe rip the sky.

With a flimsy wave of his fingers Pilate started onward, but then had a last thought. "Talk to the guards," he said, this time loud enough for me to hear.

Joseph bowed, properly, to show his gratitude.

As Pilate continued across the vast hall, he caught sight of me and looked twice as if he might know me. If he did remember me, he did not let on. I was nothing to him any longer, a widow with no influence at court. It would be beneath him to acknowledge me.

Joseph returned to the street; I followed. As we rode away, he spoke to me, sitting sideways next to his driver as before.

"He won't help, but he won't interfere," Joseph said.

We rode on, making our way to a street of shops and storage spaces not far from the hippodrome. The driver stopped in front of a little stone building with an unusually clean doorway. Joseph took a key from his pocket, opened the heavy wooden door and entered.

I followed him into a room scented by spices and fragrant oils. His driver held the door open while Joseph lit a lamp. In the growing light the room revealed all of its treasures. This was Joseph's storage space. On one side of the entrance, shelves contained lengths of fabric, neatly folded to a uniform size. On the other side there were muslin sacks filled with spices and tea leaves, or so my nose told me.

He went directly to the shelves and took down a length of flawless linen.

"From Egypt," he said, unfolding it to inspect it. The respect he showed for the exquisite cloth touched my heart. He was an artist, a man who equated beauty with heaven's bounty. He inhaled the scent of the flax, content that it was clean and of a refined quality.

Going back to the shelf, he poked through the other fabrics, ran his fingers over one or two. "This one," he said, going back to his first choice. He held it out for me to touch.

It was as soft as flower petals. I smiled. He folded the fabric expertly and put it under his arm.

We crossed the room. He went directly to a particular muslin sack and ripped open the top corner to look inside. He handed me the linen fabric he had been carrying and picked up the sack in one arm. I smelled myrrh. "From Ethiopia," he said, too preoccupied to say more.

He walked deeper into the room to a narrow staircase leading to an underground cave. I followed, and once he set the lamp on the shelf, I saw a tiny space, cool and still, with shelves sparsely dotted by jars of aromatic oils. Essence of nard and aloe were kept in simple stone containers, each sealed and kept fresh until it was put to use. Joseph knew exactly what the jars contained and chose several.

"Aloe," he said, holding the first one toward me. "The most noble of plants."

I would have said it was bland and basic, but artists have their own vision. Joseph's art was the natural world.

"Aloe has no strong odor to appeal to us," he said. "But it offers us a generous gift. What is more soothing than aloe?"

He led the way back upstairs, taking obvious pleasure in all that the storage room contained. He might have told me stories about the farms and orchards, the artisans he had met in his travels. He might have recalled a long evening spent with the weavers, the growers, the perfumers he had come to know and admire for their skills.

Another time, perhaps.

We put our linen and spices into the cart, protected by the

tarp the driver raised while we were inside the storage house. It was not raining, but threatened to do so at any moment. Joseph went back once more to be certain that everything was in order and that the lamp was fully extinguished. He came out, locked the door and cleaned away a few date pits someone had carelessly tossed as they passed by. Then he returned to the cart.

In our last stop, we entered Joseph's property. I had never seen it, a modest house with a small garden marked by thistle, bean caper and rock rose.

"My family home is Arimathea, but I have decided to be buried in Jerusalem," he offered. "I hope one day to rest in the shadow of King David's gate. Now our beloved teacher will lie in my place. But perhaps one day soon I will rest beside him. He is family to me now." The round black eyes, so often brightened by joyful pleasure, were dull with pain.

We walked past the house, through the garden, to the sound of workmen digging the track needed to roll the stone into place. We stood nearby.

"You see? This is the place," Joseph said. He couldn't help but admire the workmanship of the tomb, with its perfectly arched ceiling and precisely chiseled walls.

"Yes," I answered vaguely. We stood looking at the large rock the stonecutter and his men were busy preparing.

Joseph led us into the cave. There were two small chambers. In the first was a shallow pit encircled by benches. Beyond that was the burial chamber, where a shelf to hold a body had been cut into the wall.

Once the bones decayed, they would be taken from the shelf and placed in the ossuary that stood waiting in the corner of the room. It was some comfort to me that Jesus and Joseph might both be buried in this serene place. By his love and kindness Joseph had taken what was a shameful death in the eyes of the world and made it noble.

I placed the linen on the bench in the first room and the jar of aloe beside it. Joseph laid the sack of myrrh on the ground nearby. The sweet spicy scent began to mix with the dank odor of earth in a pleasant way.

The walk back to the Place of Skulls was the longest of my life. I stopped once to pick up a stone spattered with blood and put it in my pocket. So many had walked that path to their death, the blood might have belonged to a stranger's body, but I took it. I wanted something I could touch and hold, to remind me of this day.

Close to the top of the hill, soldiers were heaving a corpse into an open grave. One of the dead man's feet was missing. The dogs must have got to him.

Looking up at my healer, his head sunk down on his chest, I saw a soldier hurl a lance at him. It tore into the cold ribs, dangled from his side and clattered to the ground. Perhaps my cousin sent me away with Joseph because she knew me too well. Had I stayed to ponder what she must have witnessed, my young faith, already battered, might well have fled and left me to despair.

My cousin and the others stood close to the body. None

of them spoke. Joseph went to the captain, who pushed him away, then started to walk past him. He got the man's attention when he mentioned Pilate.

The other soldiers were picking up their belongings and preparing to leave the hill. The captain kept one eye on them as he listened to Joseph.

"Pilate has no objection," the spice dealer assured him.

The captain bent down to tighten his sandal, all but ignoring Joseph.

"We aren't going to wait," he snarled.

Joseph reached into his pocket and took out his coin pouch. The captain looked twice. Gold coins exchanging hands. There must have been ten at least.

"Be quick," the soldier said. "We're leaving."

So few of us remained near the cross that we women had to help carry the body. A ladder from somewhere, a lever to pry out the nails, the weight of the body as we lifted it down. My cousin was the first to take hold of her son. We left her alone with him. She rocked him gently, pressed his hair back from his lovely face. She kissed his eyes, his lips. She placed her forehead against his broken heart.

Joseph told the others what he had arranged. There was a cart waiting at the bottom of the hill, and a tomb in his garden. Then he went to Mary and spoke to her, reassuring her. I could see in his placid face that what would have been a terrible effort for me was a source of contentment for Joseph. He was in the habit of being generous.

Mary held her son. Joseph waited beside her until at last she looked up at him. All of us, together, lifted the body and carried it down the hill.

The fragrance of myrrh filled the tomb. We laid the linen cloth on the ground and placed his body there, careful not to touch his wounds for fear of being contaminated by the blood of a dead man.

We women went into the garden and quickly gathered flowers to place beneath his head and shoulders. An odd light filled the garden for a moment, as if the sun were setting on a clear evening. A ray of hope, I wanted to say out loud. But we had nothing to hope for now. By the time we returned to the tomb, twilight settled over the place.

We wrapped his head in linen, lifted him and placed the rose and bean caper beneath him. Then we laid him down on his fragrant bed and covered him with the generous linen.

The rest would have to wait. We would light our candles, wash and anoint the body, pray and sing together after the Sabbath. But we had already stayed longer than we should.

Rather than place the body on the shelf inside the burial chamber, we rested it on the bench in the entranceway, because we planned to return. When that was done, we stood together, each in our own silent prayer. Joseph began one of the ancient songs. His warm, full voice faded and wavered, but he continued. We joined him, doing our best.

In the dark, to the sound of crickets and frogs, we rolled the stone in front of the tomb, as the stonecutters had arranged. When we were finished, my cousin began to walk the length of the grave and back again. Her arms at her sides, she made a sound like no human noise I have ever heard.

She roared, a lioness grieving her loved one. Grief and rage rose up from deep within her. None of us went near.

I walked back into the garden. A woman of fragile, if eager faith, I had my own tangled emotions to contend with. All of us should have been on our way, but none of us seemed able to leave. We were stung, each of us, by the loss that the hour represented.

EPILOGUE

Now in the church at Antioch there were prophets and
teachers: Barnabas...Manaen, a member of the court
of Herod the ruler, and Saul.

—*Acts of the Apostles* 13:1

I was there the morning he rose from the tomb, but I
did not recognize him in the light. I will never truly
understand all that I saw. I go on with my life hoping that
one day more of the mysteries will become clear.

None of us was the same after my healer came back from
the grave. We got spun around, each in a new direction. I saw
it first in my cousin Mary. She was like a luminous creature
that has shed its skin. She emerged from her trials, as tender
and wise as a newborn.

For a time she was in Ephesus with John, the youngest of

her son's close followers. In his zeal he set out to tell everyone with ears about what he had witnessed in Galilee. A peculiar sort with his head in the clouds, he needed someone to keep him properly fed and dressed.

It was while Mary was away that I began to look after her house. I hadn't planned to. I had my own affairs to manage, as I had recently opened Sepphoris to travelers on their way to the Holy City. Phineas was my partner. A freed slave, he wanted to stay on and help me to manage the Inn at Sepphoris.

"Joanna, go to Nazareth." The words came back to me. Visitors to Sepphoris helped me see the meaning. They would ask about the house where the prophet was born. I showed it to them, hardly noticing at first that it was crumbling from neglect. My cousin's family had moved away, fleeing the curiosity seekers.

I was alone in the house one afternoon when an inspiring clump of plaster fell from the ceiling and brought me to my senses. The repair work began soon afterward.

My cousin came home from her travels at last. Quite by choice, she settled in a cave on Mount Olive. From the entrance to her dwelling she could see the places where her son had spent himself, lived and died and risen again. She needed time to look deeply, she said. And so she stayed.

Joseph, the spice dealer, was her loyal caretaker, as he had cared for her son in the end. I will ask him one day why he gave his own tomb as the burial place for my healer. Was it out of love for Jesus, or even more for Jesus's mother?

It was in her final days that I confided in my cousin that I did not know how to live if she was gone and I was alone without a husband. Mary listened as I spoke my heart and stroked my hand as I rambled. But her only answer was that God would provide.

One day she lay down on her mat peacefully and did not get up again. For the first time since I had known her, she was not in any pain. It was only that she was worn out from a life of extremes. She slept quietly, and at last she slipped away.

I knew her time had come when I felt the air stir around me. I watched an escort of blessed women enter and stand near her. Sarah, Ruth, Esther—I can't say how I recognized them by name. Somehow, I knew.

That was some years ago. Now, when travelers from Babylon or Egypt come to my inn, I know what to expect. They want me to show them the place where the mother goddess lived. They believe that my cousin Mary was Isis, returned to earth as a Nazarene woman. They tell me with certainty that Mary was like the sorrowful mother goddess who lost her son, Osiris, to demons. The noble son escaped from the underworld and returned to life. Is it not exactly what happened in Galilee? I am asked.

"No," I insist. "Mary was a woman not a goddess. She had no divine powers. That is the great lesson of her life. Through the darkest times she never lost her faith. She showed me what it means to be a woman of God.

I might have been content to give myself up to the work at hand. Managing the Inn at Sepphoris and the Nazareth shrine had its satisfactions. But there was Manaen. Hard as I tried, I could not give him up. To be one with my Creator is my great privilege. But I am a woman of practical needs more than high ideals.

When he went away, I was like a foreigner torn from her home. I only discovered this after we parted.

Manaen went to Antioch to help a community that wanted to learn the ways of the teacher. There were new followers by the day in cities across the Mediterranean, even as far off as Rome. He was needed in Antioch, but he had other reasons for leaving Tiberias when he did. There was no future for Manaen in Antipas's court. The tetrarch grew more vicious and deceitful by the day. It was not safe for an honorable man to be near him.

When the Romans finally banished Antipas to Gaul, I threw myself into the spring near my orchard, to wash myself of his memory.

I wrote to Manaen, too often, I suppose, in my loneliness. He answered in letters blazing with enthusiasm. Then one day he walked back into my house without so much as a word of warning. I saw him coming along the road. He was too thin, but his face had been polished and refined by his many acts of goodness.

"Your cousin, Mary…" The words trailed off. "Joseph the spice merchant brought me her message."

It was the first I heard that Mary wanted to reach Manaen. I wondered why she had not told me. She knew I would have done anything for her.

It pained me to think that a request of hers would go un-answered. My eyes flooded with tears.

"Mary asked me to return here, to Sepphoris," he said. "She thought you would need help managing the inn."

That was all some time ago. Manaen and I are old now, an old married couple. I am nearly seventy. I still have most of my teeth, but little else about me has remained the same.

TWO WOMEN OF GALILEE
QUESTIONS FOR DISCUSSION

1. Joanna clearly has mixed feelings about her life as a member of Herod Antipas's court. Does she seem to delight in the privileges or simply endure court life for the sake of her marriage, or a little of both?

2. Her husband, Chuza, gives her a certain amount of freedom in their marriage. Is this out of acceptance for her curious and restless nature, or does he seem to you unable to control her? Perhaps there are other reasons you thought of as you read?

3. Why would Joanna run away from Jesus the first time she sees him? She is in failing health, and we know she is partial to magic and mystery, yet she becomes terrified when faced with a miracle healer. How much of her fear do you think has to do with the instinctive dread of change most people feel? Perhaps she fears the unknown experience of physical health and the ways that might change her world—what changes do you think she might fear?

4. When Joanna goes to meet Mary, the mother of Jesus, she is looking for a favor. But Mary does not immediately offer help. Why is that? How much of Mary's hesitation do you think has to do with her protective feelings toward her son? Is she also trying to show Joanna how Joanna presumes superiority over others because of her social status?

5. Discuss the friendship of Mary and Joanna. What does each woman offer the other? Is one stronger than the other, or are they both strong in different ways?

6. Joanna goes through a change of heart, but it is not instant and complete in one stroke. She comes to believe in God and in Jesus slowly. Are there other experiences in life, other changes of heart, that occur in a similar way? Can you think of examples in your own life?

7. In First Century Palestine, as well as elsewhere in the Middle East, the role of a mother was one of honor. We see this in the way people flock to Mary when they want something from her son. The elder of town

comes to her and implies that she should control Jesus, silence him. Broken people, including Joanna, turn to her for help and guidance. What are the social pressures on Mary, and what privileges does she have because Jesus is a public figure? Is there anything to compare with it in modern times?

8. Joanna and her husband, Chuza, have very different religious beliefs. How does it affect their relationship? He refuses to join in her newly found faith, even after she is healed of her illness. She is disappointed in his response but doesn't persist, and he doesn't forbid her to follow her heart. Do you find their ways of dealing with the issue unusual in a married couple?

9. Who pays the highest price for Joanna's decision to become a follower of Jesus, Joanna or Chuza? What are the lessons here?

10. Joanna is surprised and her feelings are hurt when her servant, Octavia, asks for freedom. Meanwhile Phineas, another of Joanna's servants, apparently has no desire

to be freed. How do the "benefits" of the slave system, including food, shelter, clothing and basic security, conflict with the teachings of Jesus? Does Joanna understand this?

11. In three of the gospels (Matthew, Mark and Luke), there are more women followers of Jesus than men at the Crucifixion of Jesus, and women are the first witnesses to the Resurrection (in John's gospel, the resurrected Jesus appears first to Mary Magdalene alone). We know that in biblical times women and children were considered closer to the paralytics, the blind and homeless of Galilee than to the able-bodied men in the community. What are the gospel writers telling us about the inherent value of women and others of their social status? Are there also implications about the powerful and how they respond to life's mysteries?

12. Why would Mary retreat from the world the way she does toward the end of the novel?

The highly anticipated
follow-up to
The Beach House
by *New York Times*
bestselling author

Mary Alice
MONROE

It's been five years since the
original turtle lady, old
Miss Lovie Rutledge, passed
away, but her legacy lives on
with some special women,
especially Toy and her daughter,
young Little Lovie.

The turtle season begins the day
Toy rescues a sick sea turtle on
the beach. When Toy brings the
loggerhead to the aquarium, she
begins a turtle hospital with the
help of her boss, Ethan. As the
summer progresses and the sea
turtles take their measured steps
toward healing and freedom,
Toy must find her own strength
to face her fears and move
courageously toward the future.

Swimming Lessons

"An exceptional and
heartwarming work of fiction."
—*Publishers Weekly* starred
review on *The Beach House*

Available wherever books
are sold!